D0254488

THE
END
OF THE
LINE

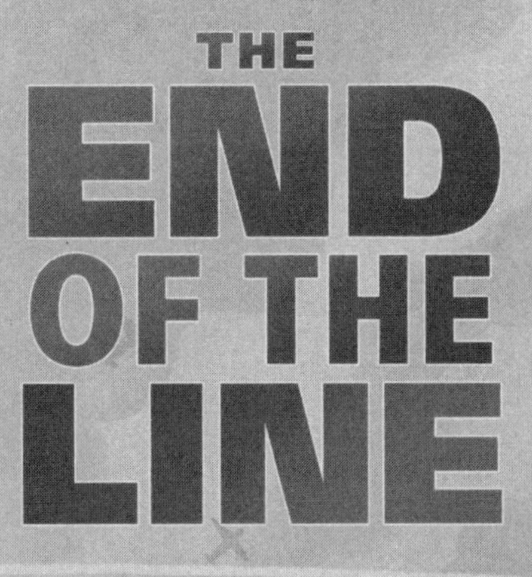
THE
END
OF THE
LINE

Sharon E. McKay

Edited by Barbara Berson
Interior designed by Monica Charny
Cover designed by Sheryl Shapiro
Tram icon used on page 4 and throughout, © iStockphoto Inc./Kathy Konkle

Annick Press Ltd.

We acknowledge the support of the Canada Council for the Arts, the Ontario Arts Council, and the Government of Canada through the Canada Book Fund (CBF) for our publishing activities.

Cataloging in Publication

McKay, Sharon E., author
End of the line / Sharon E. McKay.

Issued in print and electronic formats.
ISBN 978-1-55451-658-2 (pbk.).--ISBN 978-1-55451-659-9 (bound)
ISBN 978-1-55451-660-5 (epub).--ISBN 978-1-55451-661-2 (pdf)

I. Title.

PS8575.K2898E63 2014 jC813'.54 C2014-900172-X
C2014-900173-8

Distributed in Canada by
Firefly Books Ltd.
50 Staples Avenue, Unit 1
Richmond Hill, ON
L4B 0A7

Published in the U.S.A. by
Annick Press (U.S.) Ltd.

Distributed in the U.S.A. by
Firefly Books (U.S.) Inc.
P.O. Box 1338
Ellicott Station
Buffalo, NY 14205

Printed in Canada

Visit us at: www.annickpress.com
Visit Sharon E. McKay at: www.sharonmckay.com

Also available in e-book format. Please visit www.annickpress.com/ebooks.html for more details.
Or scan

MIX
Paper from responsible sources
FSC® C004071

For Taylor Burke

WHEN STRANGERS WERE SAVIORS

Today, children are often told, "Don't talk to strangers." Not long ago, however, strangers were thought of as rescuers.

In World War II, when the German army invaded most of Europe, concern for the safety of children resulted in millions and millions of them being hurled into the arms of strangers.

This is the story of a Jewish girl in Holland who found sanctuary in the home of two strangers. Hiding a Jewish child from the Nazis was dangerous. If the child was discovered, he or she would be sent to a prison camp, where death would almost certainly follow. The rescuers would likely be imprisoned too, and possibly killed. To save a Jewish child took great courage. These strangers would eventually be recognized for their bravery and named the "Righteous Gentiles."

CHAPTER 1

1942

Amsterdam, Fall

"You and your daughter must leave. My husband should not have brought you here."

The woman stood in her warm kitchen but shook as if she were standing out in the cold.

"I am hurrying, Mrs. Dahl." The young mother was on her knees in front of a child who was five or six years old. She did up the last button on her daughter's coat. Three, four, five layers of clothes swaddled the child. She looked like a round little ball. The child blinked, swallowed, and tried not to cry. It was a promise—not to cry. "No tears, my darling," the mother whispered into the child's ear.

"You must understand, I have children of my own to protect. My neighbors could report us. We don't know who to trust. The Nazis will kill us all if they find you here. My children ... What would *you* do?"

"Thank you for letting us stay for a few days. And thank your husband for his help." The young mother put on a light raincoat and tied a gray headscarf under her chin.

"Remember, look for the woman in the green hat. She will take your daughter to a safe place. We wish we could help you too ..." Mrs. Dahl stood behind a curtain in the window and peeked out to the road.

"I will manage. It's my daughter's safety that's important." The mother spoke so quietly that the other woman did not appear to hear.

"Please, never mention our names, never. Leave through the back garden." The woman turned and dug deep into her apron pocket. "It is seven blocks to the tram line. Here, I have tickets. Take them, please."

"Yes, goodbye." The young mother tucked the tickets into her handbag.

"For the child." The woman handed the little girl an apple. "*Geb achting*," she whispered.

"Do you speak Yiddish?" The mother was astonished.

"No ... a little ... do not ask questions ... just go, please." Mrs. Dahl sat down on a kitchen chair and put her head in her hands.

Mother and child walked out of the house, crossed the back garden, and stood at the gate.

"Mamma, is Mrs. Dahl crying?" asked the child.

"She is very sad ... and perhaps she is keeping a secret," said the mother.

At that moment they heard voices coming down the lane.

"Hide," the mother hissed as she pulled on her daughter's hand. The two crouched behind a shed and waited. The voices wafted past them and away, but still they waited.

"Mamma, what does '*Geb achting*' mean?" whispered the child.

Her mother put her finger to her lips, listened, and then spoke so quietly the child had to lean in close to hear. "It is Yiddish. It is the language of the Jews. It means 'Be careful.'"

Geb achting. Geb achting. Geb achting, the child repeated to herself.

"But Mamma, we are Jewish and we do not speak Yiddish."

"Hush! Tell no one that you are Jewish. If anyone asks you, say no. You know this." Her mother put her head in her hands, just like Mrs. Dahl.

"Don't cry, Mamma. Don't cry. I won't tell anyone."

"Come, we have to hurry." Her mother brushed away her tears and took a deep breath. "I can't very well tell you not to cry and then cry myself, can I?" Mamma gave a pained smile, the kind of smile where the mouth curls up but the eyes stay the same. She stood and took the child's hand.

"Where are we going?" The child looked up at her mother.

"Hush, darling." Her mother peered up and down the lane. When she was sure no one was watching, the two slipped out into the laneway.

"A watery sky. It looks like rain." Lars shielded his eyes and looked up into a gray sky.

Hans locked the house, then looked up to see that all the windows were closed, as was his habit. It was a pretty little house. There were two small but tidy rooms on the main floor, two small, tidy bedrooms upstairs, and a tiny, tidy room tucked under the eaves at the very top. This had once been their playroom, when they were little.

Hans and Lars Gorter were brothers. Hans was round and short—egg-like, in fact. Lars was tall and thin, like a stick, or maybe a praying mantis. They were born two years apart. Hans, at sixty-five years of age, was the elder, and Lars, the younger, was sixty-three. Neither had married. They had lived with their mamma until she'd passed away ten years ago. Papa had died when Hans and Lars were just boys. Now the two brothers lived alone, together.

They had hairy ears, rosy cheeks, and blue eyes that folded down in the corners. Their white eyebrows looked like wings about to take flight. They were honest and hardworking Dutchmen, through and through.

Before starting out for work, Hans and Lars looked across to Mrs. Vos's home, as was their habit. Her blinds were up and therefore so was she. Mrs. Vos, eighty, had been their mamma's dearest friend. To young boys who'd had no living grandparents, or indeed any living relatives, she had been auntie, granny, and friend all neatly tied up in one person. Satisfied that all was right at Mrs. Vos's house, they carried on.

There were eight pretty houses on their cul-de-sac, a road that ended in a little circle. Each house had fading flowers in the tiny front garden. Doors were painted barn red, indigo blue, sunny yellow, minty green, or plum purple. The homes were surrounded by wrought-iron fences with gates, and instead of indoor toilets most of them had privies, or outhouses, tucked in the back garden. There was a busy street at the far end of their little road. Here large trucks filled with the invading Nazi soldiers barged up and down the cobblestone roadways spewing great clouds of black smoke. Occasionally they passed German soldiers on foot. Large guns were slung over their shoulders. Their black boots made clicking sounds on the sidewalk.

The Germans had invaded their beloved Holland two years ago—on May 10, 1940, to be precise. On that day, German aircraft had raced across the sky, and the sound of the engines had so frightened Mrs. Vos that she had run across the road to the brothers' home in her nightdress. With blankets over their shoulders, the three sat around a dying coal fire in the parlor.

"The army is prepared," declared Hans.

"Yes, we will fight them off," Lars agreed. Although at his advanced age he could hardly count himself among the "we."

All three had lived through the Great War and a depression, but it was only Mrs. Vos who was not so sure that her lovely country could successfully battle the great German military machine. She nodded her head anyway as the three huddled around the dwindling fire.

The Nazi invasion was swift. In the beginning, the Nazi soldiers called themselves "brothers" of the Dutch. They paid top dollar for food and rent. The Dutch had suffered a depression for years and so the Germans' money was very welcome. At first, things seemed to be looking up. But then everything changed.

The Dutch remained loyal to their Queen Wilhelmina, who had fled to London, along with the Dutch government, when the Germans invaded. And, despite all the rules and threats issued by the Nazis, many people in Holland continued to listen to a Dutch-language news broadcast—Radio Oranje—that came from London, England. This stubbornness infuriated the Nazis.

The brothers knew of Dutch dissidents who blew up train tracks and caused trouble for the Nazis. The Nazis retaliated by arresting people, shooting many, and sending others far away to prison camps. What these camps were really like seemed to be a matter for speculation. Some people said they were terrible places. But Hans and Lars believed that the Germans might be conquerors, and this Hitler fellow might be rather awful, but in the end they were all Europeans and therefore civilized. Civilized people did not go about murdering other people. That was how they thought.

Hans and Lars carried on down the road. Life had changed in two short years. For one thing, there were sandbags everywhere—in front of buildings, around lampposts, under large windows. They wondered what they were for. If a bomb dropped, Allied or German, a sandbag here or there would not do much. It was curious.

Their once beautiful city now looked dowdy and unkempt. Everyone was fearful and afraid. Everyone was in a hurry. Smiles were rare and greetings unspoken.

Hans checked his watch. Every morning they arrived at the tram depot not a minute too early or a minute too late, as was their habit. Hans drove a city tram, although in the past foreign visitors called it a streetcar. That was curious too. There was nothing car-like about a tram.

Lars was the ticket collector. They had held these positions for forty-three years.

"Mamma, I am hot." The child, with eyes the color of chocolate and two long auburn braids tied with small ribbons hanging down her back, tried to keep up with her mother's strides, but it was hard with all the clothes she was wearing.

The woman stopped, pulled the child close, and whispered, "Rest a little. It won't be long now, my darling girl. Soon you will be safe. But remember your promise? You must not tell anyone where we have been. It would get them in trouble. Promise?"

The child bobbed her head. There were so many secrets to keep, but that one was easy. She didn't know where they'd stayed, or even where they were right at that moment.

They stopped in front of a shop window. The child cupped her hands around her eyes and peered into the store. "Look, Mamma!" She squealed with delight as she pointed to the sweets and pastries that sat like jewels on lace-covered pedestals. There were almond-coated cakes, jam-filled cookies, swirls of lemon-drop icing, and her favorite, a ginger cake called *peperkoek*. Her mouth watered and her eyes grew as big as pies. Would her mother buy her a sweet? She looked over to the entrance of the shop. She could not read yet but she knew what the ugly words brushed on the glass door with black paint said—no Jews.

The young mother didn't notice the sweets. She looked past the window display to a clock on the far wall. They still had to walk four more blocks to the tram stop, board the tram, and travel five stops. There, Mrs. Dahl had assured them, they would be met by a woman wearing a green hat. The woman would take her child to a safe haven. Everything rested on this woman—a stranger.

"Come." The mother reached out her hand and the two walked on. The child looked back at the sweets in the window but said nothing.

That day, like every day, Lars stood beside Hans at the top of the tram. While Hans concerned himself with steering through traffic, Lars surveyed the passengers.

On the right, midway down the aisle, was a middle-aged nun wearing a white-winged cornette on her head. Lars didn't have to look up to know that she was near. The gentle *click-clicking* sound of her beaded rosary, attached to her belt, announced her presence.

On the left, two seats behind Hans, Lars recognized a frequent passenger, a blond boy of perhaps sixteen or seventeen years of age, broad-shouldered, wearing the uniform of the Hitler Youth: brown shirt, short pants, knee socks, and a lanyard leading to a whistle that was tucked in his shirt pocket. Lars was familiar now with the different uniforms worn by the soldiers who had invaded his country. Brown was for the Hitler Youth; black was for the hated SS or the Gestapo; green for the police. Across the aisle from the boy sat two giggly girls. If the boy noticed them, he did not let on.

Seated behind the two giggly girls was a young woman disguised as an older woman. Did she think Lars did not notice? Lars had become a great observer of people over the years, but he was an expert on hands in particular, having taken tickets from hands for so many years. Hers were thin, soft, and without liver spots. These were the hands of a young woman.

City employees had been ordered to report odd behavior to their superiors, who would, they were told, pass the information on to "the authorities." That really meant the Nazis. This woman's behavior was certainly odd, but it had never occurred to Hans or Lars to betray a fellow countryman. Spying was a part of the job that irked them both, but then it was happening all over their country—neighbors spying on neighbors, coworkers betraying each other. It was a terrible thing, and without ever having discussed it, Hans and Lars were of the same mind: they would take no part in it.

The Nazis particularly hated Jews. The Nazis believed that Jews were the cause of great grief in the world. There was endless talk about the "master race" and how the Nazis were better than anyone else.

Hans and Lars didn't know any Jews, although Hans had once had a tooth pulled by a Jewish dentist. The man had seemed very nice. All this talk, all this hatred, was just confusing. They had seen the leaflets and the posters, and heard the ridiculous speeches on the radio—it was inescapable—but what could two old men do?

Mother and child stood at the tram stop. The young mother was nervous. It was then that the child noticed her mother's raincoat.

"Mamma, where is it?" The child touched her mother's shoulder. Jews had been ordered to wear yellow stars on their outer clothing.

"Hush, darling." Her mother's eyes widened. There were others waiting in line for the tram. Had anyone overheard? Satisfied, she bent down and whispered, "No talking until we get off the tram."

The child's mouth twitched. "I'm sorry." She might have cried had she not promised her mother that there would be no tears, no matter what. Mamma hugged her hard, rocked her back and forth, then kissed the top of her head.

The child looked over her mother's shoulder and instantly cheered up. "Look, Mamma, isn't she beautiful?" The child pointed to a faded movie poster glued onto a lamppost. It was of a woman in a magnificent dress, with silver hair piled high on her head.

"*Marie Antoinette*. It's a movie. I remember. Norma Shearer was the star. Your father took me one Christmas." The woman sighed deeply.

"What's wrong, Mamma?" The child tugged at her mother's coat.

The woman blinked, then motioned toward the on-coming tram. "Here it comes." She took the child's hand.

CHAPTER 2

Hans brought the tram to a stop and opened the door. Lars bade "*Goedemorgen*" to an elderly man, the nun with her white-winged hat, two women with shopping bags, and two students. A school was right on the tram line, so there were always students in school uniforms on the tram. A mother and child followed. He had not seen them before.

The nun took her usual seat midway down the aisle on the right. The woman and child took the seat directly behind Hans and in front of the boy in the Hitler Youth uniform. Lars was not one to notice people in particular, but he was one to observe behavior. This woman seemed very nervous. Her scarf had slipped off her head and now lay like a collar around her neck. She was thin and dark-haired, with high cheekbones and large brown eyes. Perhaps she was a ballerina, or one of those fashion models, although surely such a person would dress better.

She gripped the hand of a child who might be five or six, although Lars was no judge of a child's age.

The child had a thin face like her mother's but an oddly round, sausage-like body. He supposed this could be completely normal—to be thin on top and chubby on the bottom. Neither of the brothers had much contact with children, beyond telling the occasional boy not to stick his hand or head out the window in case it got lopped off. With the exception of their neighbor, Mrs. Vos, Lars and Hans had very few conversations with women either, the wives of the butcher and baker being exceptions.

Lars stood over the woman. "Tickets?"

She handed Lars the tickets. She did not look up. The child, however, gave him a shy smile.

"HALT!" A Nazi soldier stood on the rails directly ahead of the tram. He held up a flat palm while repeatedly yelling "Halt! Halt!" into a megaphone.

Hans, at the tram's controls, pushed down hard on the brake and pulled the emergency lever up with all his might. The wheels squealed and screeched, throwing jagged, crystal sparks out from under the tram.

Passengers lurched forward and back, straining necks and handles on handbags and packages. Lars grabbed the overhead railing and rocked on the balls of his feet. Hans, his right hand still on the emergency brake, frowned as the tram finally came to a stop and a grim Nazi soldier got on. As the war went on these intrusions were becoming more frequent, and there was no getting used to them.

Lars stood in the middle of the tram clenching his teeth as his fingers curled around the overhead bar. Every passenger on the tram seemed to tense up and hold their breath.

Lars peered out the window. There was an odd assortment of people clearing away rubble along the roadside. Some wore business suits; one had a large apron tied around his middle. There was a man in a white coat—a doctor, perhaps?—and several well-dressed women teetering on high heels. The only thing they all had in common was a gold star sewn on the right-hand side of their clothes. Lars had seen this before, Jewish citizens made to do menial jobs on the whim and command of the bully-Nazis.

Two Nazi soldiers, puffing on cigarettes, guarded them. A third held the leash of a German shepherd dog. Straining against the leather strap, the dog stood on its hind legs, pedaled its front legs in the air, and bared its teeth at one of the young women. The handler seemed to find the dog's antics amusing and egged the animal on.

Lars watched the soldier, a small man, as he positioned himself squarely at the top of the aisle and pointed his rifle at the passengers. "Papers," he barked. There was a rustle as people reached into pockets and handbags to retrieve bits of paper that had been folded and refolded a hundred, a thousand, times—until they were as soft as tissue.

The soldier stood over the Hitler Youth. "Papers," he repeated. The boy flicked an ID badge, put it back into his pocket, and looked out the window.

The soldier moved toward the young mother. Even from a distance Lars could see the mother's shoulders shaking. She whispered something to the child. She passed the child something—a pear, or an apple, perhaps. Then she inched away from the girl, as if to distance herself.

Lars watched as the soldier bore down on the young woman and her child. "Papers!" he bellowed.

Lars shifted on his feet. What to do? He could see her hands shaking as she held out a small card. He moved forward and peered over the soldier's shoulder. A red J was stamped on the cardboard identification. J stood for Jew.

His own heart began to pound. Jews had been banned from using trams. And where was her yellow star?

The soldier yelled at the woman in German and pointed to the door at the back of the tram. She stood and looked directly into Lars's eyes. The young mother's eyes were wide with terror. Lars was spellbound, his feet glued to the floor. She brushed past him.

"*Schnell, schnell!*" yelled the soldier. The woman did not look back as she walked off the tram and into the clutches of a second soldier.

Lars was confused. Wait! Did she mean to desert her child? Where were they taking her? Lars had overheard passengers talking about a camp called Westerbork. It was far away, in the northeastern Netherlands. His heart was pounding. Would this child's mother end up there? He looked through the window at the soldiers on the road, at the truck, at the dog. He put his hand to his chest, as if that would somehow make his heart stop hammering.

What to do? Lars looked back at the child. She was trembling. He looked down the aisle. The soldier was talking to the child. "*Du musst sofort mitkommen*," he said, but not nicely and not kindly.

What did that mean? Lars wracked his brain. He knew some German from school. *You have to come immediately with us.* That was what he said, Lars was sure of it, almost sure.

Lars tried to pull air into his lungs. He was a quiet man, not given to emotional outbursts. He had never spoken up before, never. Using schoolhouse German, Lars declared, "The child does not belong to that woman. She belongs to …" He paused.

The soldier stopped. Hans, still at the controls, looked up into his rearview mirror. He could see his brother's lips move.

"She belongs to me. She is my niece." Lars's voice cracked. Hans's lips puckered into a silent "O."

No one believed him. Not the old man, the young woman in disguise, the Hitler Youth, the two women with shopping bags, the girls, or the students, and certainly not the nun. A stunned silence followed.

Hans released the brake, making the tram, at a full stop, pitch forward. Lars and the soldier were the only two standing. They plunged headlong into empty seats.

Lars, like a sailor on a ship, recovered his sea legs quickly. Grunting and grumbling, the soldier staggered up and tried to grab an overhead bar. He missed and fell into the lap of the nun. She boxed his ears. He leapt up and pointed his gun at her. Her eyebrows formed a tent, her mouth turned into a colorless bud, and her eyes said *I dare you* …

Cursing, the soldier backed away from the nun, then waved his gun about like a flag. A truck covered in gray and green canvas pulled up beside the tram. The soldiers outside the tram screamed, "*Schnell! Schnell!*"

All those standing on the street—the butcher, the doctor, the women in high heels, and the young mother—were loaded onto the back of the truck. Lars could not breathe—shock seemed to pin him in place.

The driver of the truck pounded on his horn. Grumbling, the soldier stomped off the tram and climbed in. And they were gone.

The child sat. Still.

Hans put the tram into gear. The familiar *clickity-clack* of the wheels skimming the rails calmed his heart. He took deep breaths.

Lars thumped down on the seat across from the child. "What have I done?" He spoke to no one but himself, and then waited, as if expecting an answer. He looked over at the child. She was pale, her eyes wide. Her hair looked damp and lay flat against her scalp and neck. She opened her mouth as if to speak, but no sound came out.

CHAPTER 3

Imprints of the child's nose, mouth, and hands were on the window. "Mamma, Mamma, Mamma," she whispered, her breath forming little clouds on the glass. There were no tears, just big eyes peering out into the darkening sky.

Three hours had passed since her mother had been taken away. Lars checked on her often. That is to say, he looked at her often. What should he say? An apple sat in her lap. "Would you not like to eat your apple?" he asked. She said nothing. He offered her part of his lunch, a pickled egg. She nodded politely, then nibbled on it like a little rabbit.

The tram pulled into the depot. Despite being very fussy about the state of their tram—they took great care with the sweeping, polishing, and checking of the electrics—Hans and Lars completed their duties in record time.

The child sat in her seat, holding the apple, swallowing hard over and over. Hans and Lars stood by the tram's controls and considered. Lars might have taken this time to ask the child if she had any family. Was there some place they could take her? Perhaps a father, brother, sister, or grandparent awaited her return? He could have asked these questions, and more, but he did not. He remained locked in shock.

Hans might reasonably have used this moment to be angry with his brother for being so foolish as to challenge a Nazi soldier, but it did not occur to him. Never, not even when they were boys, had they said a cross word to each other.

They had put off the decision long enough. Lars took a deep breath and spoke in a low, quiet voice. "What should we do?"

Hans had been thinking about this for some time. "We could take her to the Lost and Found Department," he whispered. For a moment they both breathed a sigh of relief, until Lars asked, "Do they take people?" Neither knew the answer. What did it matter? The Lost and Found was closed.

And then a new idea. "We shall take her to Mrs. Vos!" suggested Lars.

"Yes! Mrs. Vos will know what to do," Hans agreed.

They immediately cheered up. Mrs. Vos had been born in the minty-green house across the road from their own little house, eighty years ago. She had been married. Alas, within days of their marriage, her husband had promptly caught influenza and died. She had no children of her own, but she was once a girl, and that had to count for something!

Lars said to the child, "Come, now. We are at the end of the line." She looked terribly hot to him, rather sweaty, which was curious given that there was a chill in the air.

The little girl, who had yet to say a word, slid out of the seat, followed Lars, and stepped down out of the tram onto the cement floor of the tram depot. Weary-looking trams lined the dark tracks. She gazed up to bald, dim lights hanging from a vaulted ceiling. Her eyes widened, her lips quivered, she crossed her legs. This was a scary place.

Hans and Lars walked out of the depot fully expecting the child to follow, which she did not. Instead she stood still, legs still crossed. Lars and Hans shuffled back toward the girl.

"We have to leave now," Hans said, gently.

"I have to go pee-pee," she whispered.

Pee-pee? They thought for a moment. Ah! Yes. Of course they knew where the women's toilet was—hadn't they directed thousands, perhaps millions, there over the many decades? They had just never *been* there.

"It's down that hallway," whispered Lars.

"Yes, I know," Hans whispered back, although there was no need to whisper. There were no more than a dozen or so people milling about the entire depot. And so the three set off down the hall.

They stood at the door. "It's in there," said Lars. He pointed.

The child didn't move.

Both men shifted on their feet. "Shall I hold your apple?" asked Lars.

The child considered. She searched his face with two big brown eyes as if trying to see inside him. And then she gave it to him. "It's for my mamma, when she comes back," she said solemnly. Lars nodded and put it in his pocket. Still, the child pondered.

"Can you go in by yourself?" asked Hans. What would they do if she said no?

"Mamma doesn't let me go into a public toilet alone," said the child.

What to do? "Men are not allowed in there," whispered Lars. They were close to panicking.

"Can I help?" A glamorous woman wearing a fur collar, high-heeled shoes, and startling red lipstick stopped and gazed at the three. She looked amused.

"Our … niece … needs to … and we …" Lars stumbled over every word.

The woman laughed. "Come along, sweetheart." She held out her hand. It was only when the toilet door closed that both men realized that the woman spoke Dutch with a German accent.

Hans slumped against the wall. Lars dabbed his forehead with a large handkerchief. They waited, and waited. The child and woman finally emerged, both smiling.

"Enjoy your evening, Beatrix," she said.

Beatrix?

“Thank you,” said Beatrix.

“You are very welcome, my dear.” She beamed at Beatrix, then turned and faced the brothers. “Your niece is a delightful child, such a pretty face. But I do believe she may be coming down with something. She seems hot.” The woman placed the back of her hand on the child’s forehead. And with those words the woman glided down the hallway and took the arm of a man dressed in black.

Sweat beaded on Lars’s forehead. Hans took in a deep, halting breath. The color drained from their faces. The man was wearing the uniform of an SS officer.

“Come … Beatrix.” Lars motioned to the child. The three left the station.

Hans and Lars came to a large street, waited for the traffic signal to turn green, and started out. They were midway across the intersection when Lars turned around. Beatrix had stopped on the curb.

“Hans, Hans!” Lars hustled back to the child. Hans quickly followed. “What is wrong?” Lars asked Beatrix. She whispered something that neither could hear. Lars and Hans bent down.

Beatrix stood on tiptoes. “I’m too little to cross a busy street by myself.”

Hans and Lars shared a glance. What to do? They stood on the street corner, confused and befuddled. It was Beatrix who solved the problem. She stepped between Hans and Lars, reached up, and slipped her hands into theirs. For the first time in their lives Lars and Hans felt a small, warm hand holding their own. To Lars it was as if the curl of a wave had come to rest in his palm. To Hans it felt as if the gentlest creature on earth—a baby bird, perhaps—had nestled in his hand. In that moment both felt the intense pride that comes with great responsibility as they guided the child safely across the street.

CHAPTER 4

The two brothers and Beatrix turned off the main street and onto their own little cul-de-sac.

Standing tall, with their ties straight, the brothers approached Mrs. Vos's door. Hans knocked.

Mrs. Vos, wearing a shaggy shawl over a simple housedress, opened the door. She was old, Beatrix thought. Once, she and mamma had run to a house. Mamma had said that she knew the lady there, that the lady would give them a place to sleep. But she chased them away with a broom. That lady had worn a shawl too. Beatrix quickly stepped behind Lars.

"*Goedenavond*, Hans, and the same to you, Lars." Mrs. Vos greeted both men with a smile.

Hans was about to respond with "Good evening" as well when Mrs. Vos shifted a bit and peered around Lars.

"Who is this?" Surprise replaced the smile, and then came a furrowed brow, followed by a look of astonishment.

Lars cleared his throat. "Good evening, Mrs. Vos. This little girl was left on our tram. We wondered if you would take her in." Lars spoke plainly and confidently. He expected to hear, "Oh, do bring her in. Yes, of course I can look after her."

Instead he heard, "Left on a tram! Is she an umbrella? An overdue library book? A glove? A lunch box? A pocket-book or a bag of groceries? What do you mean, LEFT ON A TRAM?"

Good heavens, Mrs. Vos was clearly upset. Lars and Hans sputtered and twisted as if caught in a sudden, high wind.

Mrs. Vos peered down at the child and, shaking her head, said, "Take her to your house. I will come by immediately."

Glum-faced, Hans and Lars and Beatrix scurried across the road. Hans unlocked the door with the large, black key. Once inside, Hans and Lars hung up their coats and removed their hats. They folded their scarves and placed their gloves in cubbies that their dear, departed mother had put there for just that purpose.

The child looked back and forth, up and down. Her lips seemed to flutter. Her eyes watered up. Lars nudged Hans. Oh dear, they simply would not know what to do with a crying child!

"May I take your coat?" Hans spoke to the child as if she were an invited guest at a tea party. The child nodded.

Under Beatrix's coat was another, thinner coat. Perplexed, but not one to ask personal questions, Hans hung this coat up as well. Lars and Hans watched in astonishment as the child removed a sweater, and then another sweater, then another dress, and then another dress and a blouse and two skirts. There were trousers, leggings, stockings, and something that looked like shorts.

Lars and Hans pinned themselves to the wall. What to do? Stop, stop! *Oh my, oh my!*

Beatrix soon stood in a little dress appropriate for a summer picnic or a boat ride. Brightly colored clothes swam around her ankles. Only then did Lars realize that the child was not chubby at all. In fact, she was a skinny little thing with knobby elbows and knees. The child must have been terribly hot, which explained her damp hair and flushed face.

Lars took a deep breath. He cleared his throat. "Beatrix, my name is Lars Gorter, and this is my brother, Hans Gorter." Lars poked himself in the chest and then Hans in the arm. Hans bowed.

"Hello," said Beatrix.

CHAPTER 5

"Where did you come from, child?" asked Mrs. Vos.

True to her word, Mrs. Vos had come flying across the road. She now stood in the parlor, having replaced her housedress with a sturdy but suitable visiting dress. Mrs. Vos was a stickler for proper attire and good manners.

Beatrix twisted her dress with her fingers. Was this lady nice or mean? It was hard to tell.

"What is your name, child?" asked Mrs. Vos.

"Her name is Beatrix," said Lars, but very, very quietly.

"Beatrix, well, that's a lovely name," said Mrs. Vos, but not kindly. She might as easily have said, "That cabbage looks fresh."

The child remained silent.

"If you do not know where you are from, do you know where you were going? Speak up, child."

Beatrix seemed to shrink right before their eyes. She hung her head and glued her eyes to the floor. "Mamma said …" she whispered.

"Go on, what did your mother say?" asked Mrs. Vos. The child would not raise her head. A tear dribbled down her face.

"Mrs. Vos …" Lars wanted to tell Mrs. Vos that perhaps she was being a bit too harsh. But it appeared that Mrs. Vos was cross with them as well. This had never happened to them before. "She … her mother was on the tram. The Nazis boarded and …" Lars sputtered. He lost his nerve. Mrs. Vos had considerable authority over the two brothers. It was difficult for either of them to stand up to her, let alone correct her.

"I was on the tram with my mamma but bad men took her away and now I am here." Tears rimmed the girl's eyes and her nose was runny. She balled up her fist and made a mess of her face.

"Dear, dear." Hans pulled a great handkerchief the size of a pillowcase out of his pocket. He held it out with two pinched fingers. It stayed there, swaying as if caught in a slight wind. When the child made no move to take it, Hans balled the hanky up and dabbed the child's face as one might blot a wet spot on a table.

"Her papers … she is …" Lars simply could not get the words out.

"Oh, for goodness sake, Hans." Mrs. Vos grabbed the hanky and cleaned up the child's face in short order. That was when she understood. The realization spread across her face like a rash.

Mrs. Vos looked again at the child's clothes on the floor. Then, rotating in a half circle like a great battleship turning in a harbor, she addressed Hans and Lars. "Her mother was taken off the tram because she is Jewish, correct?"

Both men nodded.

"Do you not read the newspapers? The Nazis could shoot you for harboring a Jewish child."

It was Lars who whispered, "She is our … niece?"

"Your niece? I have known you all of your lives. Do you have a sister? Do you have a cousin? Do you have any living relatives?"

Neither responded.

Mrs. Vos stood very, very still. Her eyes narrowed and her lips pursed. She leaned forward and motioned to Hans and Lars to do the same. In a hushed huddle she whispered, "Do you not see the people pushing carts down the road with all their belongings? Nazis are confiscating Jewish homes and all their possessions. There is a rumor that many Jews are going into hiding. Maybe this child was being taken someplace to hide. No doubt a suitcase would have been noticed, so this child's mother dressed her in all the clothes she owned."

Hans and Lars stood back. Neither spoke, but each could hear the other thinking. Of course they had seen things—on the road mostly, from the tram's windows—people walking with suitcases and such. And they knew some of the rules, how could they not? Rules were posted all over the city. Jews were not allowed in theaters, on trains, or on trams. They could not swim in public pools. They were allowed to shop for only two short hours in the afternoon, and only in certain shops, and … the list was endless. They just didn't know what they could do about it.

As for the child, what did it matter to them if she was Jewish or not? They had offered a poor child shelter for a night in much the same way they might have fed a stray cat. What else could they have done? Only monsters would have left her to sleep on the tram.

Mrs. Vos turned her attention back to the child. "Do you have any family? Anyone?"

The child shook her head. Hans and Lars, who seemed to have shrunk into boys, stood clasping and unclasping their hands.

"What is your mother's name?" she asked.

"Mamma," whispered the child.

"And I suppose that your father's name is Papa," said Mrs. Vos.

Beatrix nodded.

"And do you have a last name?" asked Mrs. Vos.

Beatrix shook her head and in a tiny voice whispered, "Mamma says not to tell."

Mrs. Vos frowned and turned to face Hans and Lars (although in truth she would have had to stand on a small stool to look Lars in the eyes). "I do not believe that you understand the danger you have put yourselves in," said

Mrs. Vos. She paused. "I am assuming that no one saw you take the child off the tram." Hans and Lars dithered. Mrs. Vos looked from one face to another. "What is it?" she demanded.

"There was a woman, in the toilet, and an SS officer, and ..." Lars stopped.

Mrs. Vos thumped down on a chair. "Start from the beginning."

It was Hans who explained it all, and when he was done Mrs. Vos shook her head and said, "The child was in your care for five minutes and you ran into an SS officer." She took a deep breath. "Well, we can only assume that the woman either did not notice that the child was wearing many layers of clothes or took pity. But understand how risky this is and how easily you can be caught." Hans and Lars turned as white as milk. Mrs. Vos pressed a finger to her lips.

"There is nothing to do now except carry on. The child needs food and sleep. Hans, I suggest you make dinner. Sausages are on the menu, I believe. And Lars, after she has eaten she must be made ready for bed."

Hans and Lars stared wide-eyed at the woman. They could not have been more confused. They were good men, kind men, but nothing in their lives had prepared them to care for a child—even if it was for only one night.

Lars began, "We were wondering if you might ..."

Mrs. Vos's flat palm was now directly in front of his face. "She is *your niece*, so you might begin by learning about how one cares for a child. I suggest that while Hans makes dinner, you remove her hair ribbons and give her hair a good brushing."

The two men stood still.

"Oh for heaven's sake. Lars, go upstairs and get me your mother's hairbrush. I am sure it is just where she left it."

Lars, delighted to escape, if only for a moment, bounded up the stairs.

By the time Lars was back, the sausages were sputtering in the frying pan, Beatrix was eating a piece of buttered bread, and her hair was fanned across her back. Lars let out a stream of air. What were they to do with all that hair? They themselves were mostly bald.

"All right, Lars, give it a try," said Mrs. Vos.

Lars held the brush between thumb and finger.

"Lars, brush," commanded Mrs. Vos.

With a quivering hand, Lars waved the brush over the child's head.

"Good heavens. It is a hairbrush, not a wand." Taking the brush in hand, Mrs. Vos gave Beatrix's hair a half dozen stiff strokes.

Beatrix was not the least bit interested in what was going on behind her back. The bread was delicious. She looked over at the loaf of bread on the cutting board. Could she save some bread for Mamma?

Mrs. Vos stopped very suddenly, the brush poised in her hand. She stood back and looked at the child's spine. A series of tiny knobs poked through the thin summer dress. Mrs. Vos sat down on a kitchen chair. Tears came to her eyes. A lump formed in her throat. Clearly, the child was starving.

"Are you unwell?" asked Lars. There was alarm in his voice.

"I am fine, thank you," Mrs. Vos whispered as she gazed at the clothes strewn on the floor, then back at the child's hair. The child was clean, her hair soft. Even from this distance she could see that the child's clothes were well mended and clean too. Keeping clean on the run, surrounded by war, without a home, must have been very, very hard. "This child is loved," she whispered.

"Pardon?" said Hans.

"Hush now, let me think." She waved Hans away. Mrs. Vos was not a woman to give in to her emotions, not when there was work to be done, and in an instant she knew what that work entailed. "We were very lucky with that woman and the SS officer, but we cannot depend on luck," she declared.

Hans and Lars glanced at each other hopefully. She had said "we."

"The neighbors have seen this child enter the house," Mrs. Vos went on.

Lars was confused. With one exception, they knew everyone on their cul-de-sac. That exception was a young woman named Lieve van der Meer, who seemed very pleasant. "Surely no one would report anything as innocent as a child coming to spend the night?" said Lars.

"These are dangerous times," said Mrs. Vos as she stood and secured the child's hair with a ribbon. "And another thing. Never let a child go to bed with unbound hair. If you do, you will both pay for it in the morning." Mrs. Vos picked up her handbag. "I will be back. Meanwhile, after you have eaten, make sure her teeth are cleaned and find her some nightclothes," ordered Mrs. Vos with the commanding voice of a general.

Hans and Lars stood mouths agape in amazement. Had Mrs. Vos suggested that the child be roasted and eaten with peas, the men could not have been more shocked.

CHAPTER 6

Mrs. Vos stepped out of the house and stood for a moment at the garden gate. She gazed up at the gray sky, then down at the little pools of rainwater that had collected among the road's cobblestones. If the road had been overhead and the sky below her feet, the world could not have felt more upside down. How could all this be happening? She had never really hated anyone, not until that moment. Now she hated the Nazis. Most of all, she hated what she had to do next.

It was early evening, seven o'clock, and the curfew imposed by the insufferable Nazis was but an hour away. Every window was covered by blackout curtains, presumably to prevent the Allies from dropping bombs on their heads. The British, the Australians, and the Canadians, all the Allies, were trying to bomb the airstrips, the harbor, and the office buildings held by the Nazis, but their aim was not always that good. What kind of war was it when your friends bombed you and your enemies tried to make traitors out of half the citizens and shoot the rest? *Humph.*

A flicker of a curtain in the window at number 3 caught her attention. Fine, she would begin there.

The raps on the door were short and crisp. A round, short fellow answered.

"Good evening, Mrs. Vos. Please, enter." Mr. Van Engle's voice spilled out and into the open air.

Good heavens, thought Mrs. Vos, *that revolting Hitler will hear the man all the way in Berlin.*

Mrs. Vos stepped inside. "How kind, Mr. Van Engle, but I require just a moment of your time. I wonder if you noticed that Lars and Hans Gorter at number 2 have welcomed their niece into their midst." Her voice was light and tinkly, very ladylike, in fact.

"Yes, I did see the child. And you say she is their *niece*?" His laughter sounded like a snort.

Mrs. Vos ignored his reaction. "Yes, that is what I just said. A *distant* niece." Mrs. Vos stared hard at the man. His laughter hung in the air like wet laundry on a line. "However, I did not come about the dear little girl who has lost both her parents. No, I came to assure you that your secret is safe with me. I did not want you to worry." She smiled.

"My secret? Whatever do you mean?" Mr. Van Engle was more than perplexed; he was aggravated. He knew, everyone knew, that it was nothing to turn a neighbor in to the Nazis, nothing at all. One could write a note to Gestapo headquarters and say, "Mr. So-and-So is a Communist" or "a homosexual" or "listens to the British broadcasts." Anything, really. The next thing you knew a truck would be at your door and off you'd go, maybe for questioning, or maybe forever.

"Mr. Van Engle, are you paying attention?" asked Mrs. Vos.

Mr. Van Engle coughed. "Yes, go ahead."

"I just wanted you to know that the Nazis will not hear it from me that your grandmother was Jewish." There was no smile this time, just a long, penetrating stare.

"My grandmamma was not Jewish." His eyes widened.

"Oh, indeed she was, on your father's side, lovely woman. What was that delicious cookie recipe she gave me? Oh dear, one's memory does wander. Each cookie was shaped in a triangle to remind one of a three-cornered hat worn by some fellow named Haman. I recall the name—Purim *kichel*! That's it. I bet you remember it too. Children do like their granny's cookies."

Mr. Van Engle sputtered in protest.

Mrs. Vos raised a finger to her lips, lowered her voice, and whispered, "Just remember, secrets can be kept, and I will keep yours." She gave a slight nod, said goodbye, and again stood on the street. The door behind her closed gently.

Mrs. Vos looked up and down before settling on the house at number 5.

Within the half hour, five houses on the road had received a visit from Mrs. Vos. All had been assured that their secret affairs, connections with the Communist Party, and flirtations with the religious group called the Jehovah's Witnesses would remain forever locked away in a letter written by Mrs. Vos and hidden in some secret location. Her parting words were the same every time: "And I am sure you will greet the niece of Hans and Lars warmly."

The last house, at number 8, belonged to Mrs. Lieve van der Meer, a woman of perhaps thirty who had moved onto the street just a year ago. Mrs. Vos and Mrs. van der Meer had traded niceties many times, and Mrs. Vos liked the younger woman immensely.

Lieve van der Meer passed her door every Sunday on her way to church. They both belonged to the same Catholic church, although Mrs. Vos was not a regular churchgoer. But not one to let an opportunity pass, and in these hard times knowing one's neighbors was important, Mrs. Vos occasionally joined Mrs. van der Meer on her walk to church. That was how Mrs. Vos learned, for example, that Lieve van der Meer worked for the Ministry of Education, was from Belgium, and had married a Dutchman. But there was no husband in sight. Mr. Van Engle, who could be trusted to spread gossip, suggested that Lieve van der Meer's husband had run off to join the British air force.

Mrs. Van Bleek, another neighbor, had said something about Lieve van der Meer's husband dying in an explosion. No one knew for certain because the information was not offered, and it would have been rude to ask. In Mrs.

Vos's mind, Mrs. van der Meer was not secretive, she was private—there was a difference.

Besides, she reminded Mrs. Vos of her younger self … well, if Mrs. Vos had been tall, blond, and blue-eyed with a trim figure. No, it wasn't a physical resemblance that Mrs. Vos recognized, it was simply that Lieve Van der Meer had an air of honesty about her.

What Mrs. Vos was sure about, almost sure, was that Lieve could be trusted. It was a feeling, an intuition. If she was wrong about her, all their lives would be at risk. Everything now depended on Mrs. Vos's instincts.

Mrs. Vos rapped at number 8. The door opened.

"Why, Mrs. Vos, how nice to see you," said Mrs. Lieve van der Meer. Her blond hair bounced off her shoulders and her smile reached up to her eyes.

"Good evening, Mrs. van der Meer. Are you alone?" It was an intrusive question. Mrs. Vos had the good manners to blush.

Lieve was not offended by the question. In fact, there might have been a hint of amusement. "Yes, of course. Do come in," she replied.

"Good," said Mrs. Vos as she stepped over the threshold. "Curfew is in twenty minutes. I will get right to the point. Lars and Hans Gorter at number 2 have rescued a little Jewish girl. She looks to be five, perhaps six years of age. They need your help."

Mrs. Lieve van der Meer paused before saying, "Under the circumstances, perhaps you might call me Lieve."

CHAPTER 7

Mrs. Vos sat in Lieve van der Meer's parlor. "Would you take a cup of coffee?" asked Lieve.

"No, thank you." Everyone offered coffee but most likely it would have been ersatz coffee, an awful substitute. In Mrs. Vos's opinion, it was better to drink mud.

The reality of just how big a chance she had taken in confiding in this young woman, a virtual stranger, was now setting in. Mrs. Vos, who was never at a loss for words, was at a loss for words.

"Hans and Lars are kindhearted. But they can't manage on their own ..."

"I think I can help. I used to be a teacher," said Lieve.

"And where did you teach?" Mrs. Vos jumped at the chance to learn more about her new friend.

"In Rotterdam. My sisters and I were born in Denmark, but then we moved to Rotterdam several years ago."

Mrs. Vos took a deep breath. The city core of Rotterdam had been bombed into oblivion by the Nazis shortly after the invasion.

"I was a schoolteacher, and a Sunday school teacher too," said Lieve.

"And where is your family now?" asked Mrs. Vos.

"I no longer have a family." Lieve looked around the room, then down at her hands. She took a deep breath, and then continued. "They died together in the bombing. I was out at the time, and when I came home our house, and everyone in it—parents, sisters, their children, my brothers-in-law, a grandfather—were gone as well. The entire street was reduced to rubble," said Lieve. She sat straight and tall as if trying to steel herself against the memory. While tears flooded her eyes, there was no self-pity in her voice.

"I am so very, very sorry. But your husband ..."

Lieve shook her head. "My husband is not here. He is doing war work."

War work? Whatever could that mean? thought Mrs. Vos. Having heard about Lieve's family, it seemed inappropriate to press the poor young woman for more information.

Mrs. Vos returned to number 2, entered without knocking, walked into the kitchen, and looked at the little scene before her. Two old men and a small child gazed back, each in their own way looking confused and frightened. What to do? She let out a long sigh and sat at the table.

"Beatrix will begin her Catholic religious education with Mrs. Lieve van der Meer at her home on Saturday morning. A niece of yours would be Catholic, and we don't want her to be tripped up by religious questions from the authorities. On Sunday we will go to church. We will all need the help of the Lord if we are to stay safe during these dangerous times."

Lars and Hans were speechless. Mrs. Vos continued. "We must trust someone. Raising a child is difficult at the best of times, or so I have heard."

The words *raising a child* resounded around the kitchen. Both Hans and Lars appeared shocked. Men could not raise a child. That was woman's work.

"We do not intend to keep her," said Hans.

Mrs. Vos sat up straight and stretched her neck, like a rabbit popping out of a rabbit hole. "What do you intend to do with her, then? Throw her into the hands of the Nazis? How will you find her mother? If you go to the authorities and ask after her, you will only draw attention to yourselves and the child." Mrs. Vos stared them both down. "Now Saturday and Sunday are taken care of. What do you plan to do with the child for the rest of the week?"

"We will take her to work with us tomorrow," said Lars.

"Perhaps her mother will have returned by then," added Hans.

"And if she does not return?" Mrs. Vos was clearly tired.

"Then we will take her to work with us every day until she does come back," said Lars.

Mrs. Vos shook her head and sighed. "Very well. I will return in the morning and show you how to braid her hair. Make sure the blackout curtains are pulled tight. You don't want to give a soldier or policeman a reason to knock on your door. Good night."

Lars walked Mrs. Vos to the door. "Thank—" he began.

"Don't thank me." She held up her hand as if holding back traffic. And then she looked down the hall and into the kitchen. Beatrix was sitting at the table, perched on the edge of her seat. "How could the mighty German army feel threatened by such a sweet child? It's madness," she added sadly.

It was past curfew. She walked out into the pitch-darkness. After looking carefully left and right, Mrs. Vos, for all her eighty years, made a dash across the road.

Through all of this talk Beatrix had sat silently. She had heard them—they'd said that mamma would come back for her tomorrow. *Mamma, mamma, come back. Find me.* She wanted to smile, laugh even, but the sausage had turned into a hard ball in her tummy.

Hans went off in search of suitable nightwear while Lars gathered up the child's clothes, still lying in a heap by the door. Pity that under all that clothing a nightgown had not been included.

"I have found one of Mother's." Hans charged back into the kitchen and held up a flannel nightgown that could have done service as a ship's sail. Hans, who could darn socks, mend holes, and hem pants, took up the scissors and chopped off half the gown, held it up to the light, then did it again and again.

Snip, snip, snip, snip. Pause. *Snip, snip, snip, snip.* Pause.

It was a peculiar-looking thing in the end. Hans and Lars turned their backs as Beatrix pulled the oddly shaped garment over her woolly undershirt and baggy flannel underpants.

"Ready," she said. Hans and Lars turned around. Oh dear.

Snip, snip, snip, snip. Pause. *Snip, snip, snip, snip.* Pause.

It was still too big, and now it was lopsided, but it would do for the night.

There was a visit to the privy at the back of the garden (Hans and Lars stood outside and guarded the door), a wash at the sink, tooth powder mixed and teeth scrubbed with a clean finger, before all three solemnly walked up a flight of stairs to Mother's old bedroom. Beatrix slipped into the big feather bed with the brass bedframe.

"*Slaap lekker,*" said Hans with a little bow.

"Sleep well," repeated Lars with a nod of the head.

They closed the door behind them. That had not been so hard. Why did people make such a fuss about raising children? All one had to do was feed them, find them something to wear, take care of the odd bits like brushing hair and teeth, and put them to bed.

They were pleased, positively jubilant. They might have slapped each other on the back had they been the sort of men to do so.

They pressed their ears to the door expecting to hear the gentle purr of a sleeping child.

Beatrix lay in the big bed. She had never been in a bed so big. The last year had been spent hiding in a cupboard or under a bed, or in an attic. She had felt safe because Mamma was there. Mamma sang to her, told her stories. Now she was alone in a big brass bed, but where was Mamma?

Mamma, Mamma, will you come back tomorrow? Please come back. She didn't mean to cry. Mamma had told her not to. People might hear. Mamma had said, "*You can't tell anyone that you are Jewish. You can't tell anyone where we lived. You must keep the secret. And you must not cry. Promise.*" It scared her when Mamma talked like that, when Mamma looked at her with big eyes. It scared her most when Mamma cried in her sleep.

Beatrix had learned to push her tears down, down into her tummy. But tonight they wouldn't stay down! The cries raced up her throat, filled her mouth, and spilled out into the air. "Mamma, Mamma," she sobbed into her pillow.

What was this? Hans and Lars, standing on the other side of the door, heard her cries.

What to do? Hans wrung his hands. Lars paced up and down the little passageway. Just a moment ago it had all seemed so easy.

They waited. Perhaps she would drift off quickly. Time passed and still the child cried. Would she not run out of tears? How many tears did a child have? A cup? A pint? A gallon?

Hans cracked opened the door. "Beatrix, are you all right?" he whispered.

What response could she give? She was six years old in a strange house, without her mother.

What to do? Hans and Lars slipped quietly into the room and stood at the bottom of the bed. They rocked on their heels for a bit before coming up with an idea.

"Perhaps she would like a toy?" suggested Lars.

"Yes, a toy!" said Hans. He bolted out of the room and flew up to the top floor of the house. He soon returned with a large, black metal train engine. It had been one of his favorite toys. Hans offered it to the child. She gulped, but still the tears rolled down her face. Not knowing what to do with it, Hans tucked it in beside her. The metal bits were pointy and cold.

Still the child cried. Her little eyes were now rimmed red.

"Perhaps we could read a story," said Hans.

"Yes, a story!" said Lars as he lurched across the hall to their own bedroom only to return with a wonderful book his mamma had given him, *The History of the Automobile.*

He read out loud the entire chapter on automobiles in the Edwardian era. He even showed her the diagrams. "Look, it used a planetary transmission, and had a pedal-based control system," he said while holding up the book.

Still the child cried. What to do? What would their own mother have done?

Old memories came back. Dusty memories that were full of holes … of when they were sick, when Lars fell off his bike, when Hans had a flu so terrible the priest had to be called. What had Mother done? Ah! They remembered. When all seemed lost Mother would lie down beside them and whisper sweet words of comfort.

Hans wrung his hands. Lars continued to pace up and down in the tiny space between the bed and the wall.

Hans, being the elder, took the lead. He lay on top of the covers on one side of the child. Lars lay on top of the covers on the other side of the great bed. They clasped their hands over their bellies and glued their eyes to the ceiling. They lay like two giant bolster pillows—one round and soft, one long and not-so-soft. Now, what were the words Mother had whispered?

"Hush, hush," said Hans to the ceiling.

"Yes, hush, hush," repeated Lars to the same ceiling.

Minutes passed. The child's cries turned to sobs and the sobs to whimpers. Beatrix wiggled and snuggled down, her arm flung carelessly over the train engine.

"Hush, hush," whispered Hans.

"Hush, hush," whispered Lars.

Many, many more minutes passed. At last she slept.

Relief spread from their heads to their toes. Slowly, Hans and Lars tiptoed out of the room. Then they hurried across the hall and threw themselves into their own bedroom. What about the dishes in the kitchen? Surely they could not leave an untidy kitchen. But exhaustion had overcome them. Without uttering a word they donned nightshirts, socks, and caps and slipped into the twin beds that their dear parents had bought for them when they were small. It took a good while before both drifted off to sleep. And sleep they did, soundly.

Hans woke first. From his bed by the window he pulled back the blackout curtain. He turned, and a small and unexpected cry popped out of his mouth.

"Lars!" Hans whispered. Lars woke up with a start. "Look." Hans pointed to the space between their twin beds.

There, on the floor, was a small lump of blankets. And underneath the blankets, curled up like a kitten, was Beatrix.

CHAPTER 8

They did their best. Years later that is exactly what Mrs. Vos would repeat, "You did your best." That morning, however, she stood on the kitchen threshold and bellowed, "What have you done?"

With hairbrush in hand, Lars stood behind Beatrix. The child was eating her breakfast. "It is a bird's nest!" Mrs. Vos railed. Among hair that stood on end were four messy braids, possibly five if one counted the knotted bit that trailed down her back.

"And what is this?" Mrs. Vos looked over at the table. On top of the flowered oilcloth was bread with the apple syrup called *appelstroop*, cheese, cold meats, peanut butter, and the chocolaty sprinkles called *hagelslag*, along with the homemade jam that Hans kept for special occasions. Plus there were biscuits, buttered slabs of a spiced cake called *ontbijtkoek*, cream cakes, currant buns, and a big mug of coffee, real coffee! Mrs. Vos was astonished. There was a war on!

"If the child eats all this, she will be sick! And good heavens, take away the coffee."

Hans, standing in front of the stove, looked surprised at first, then very glum. He opened his mouth to say … alas, he had no chance to get a word out. Mrs. Vos again raised a flat hand. Hans clamped his mouth shut.

She took the hairbrush from Lars's hand and went to work. Once the hair was brushed and properly braided, it was time to think about clothes for Beatrix. A dress (and all the necessary undergarments), socks, shoes, coat, and hat were sorted out. Three lunches were packed. And then Mrs. Vos marched them out the door.

"The apple for Mamma!" cried Beatrix. Lars pulled it out of his pocket to show her. Beatrix nodded, and Lars returned it to his pocket.

Hans took out his key.

"Never mind, I will lock up," said Mrs. Vos. "Off you go." She waved them away. Exhausted, Mrs. Vos collapsed in the chair by the window, the cup of coffee clasped in her hand.

They walked the six blocks to the tram depot. For the first time in their lives, Hans and Lars were late for work.

All day, Beatrix sat in the seat behind Hans, the driver. Holding the apple in her hand, she waited and waited and waited. Lars watched her. It hurt his heart to see the child in such pain.

Mamma did not come back.

CHAPTER 9

1943
Amsterdam, Spring

Hans pulled the pins out from the hem while keeping an eye on the scrambled egg in the frying pan. Beatrix stood on the table and tried her best not to fidget. This was the third skirt Uncle Hans had let down this month.

"There, it's as long as it will get now. Down you go, careful."

Beatrix held onto Uncle Hans's hand, stepped off the table onto a chair, and jumped to the floor.

"We have enough coupons for a half pound of butter," said Lars, who sat at the other end of the table sorting out the week's ration coupons. Food was still available but not plentiful.

"Then we shall bake a cake!" announced Hans.

Hans served the breakfast: an egg scrambled in milk

and shared among the three, an apple cut into thirds, a thin slice of bread each, and for Beatrix a mug of hot chocolate. War or no war, Hans always managed to find a special treat for Beatrix's breakfast.

As best they could, Hans and Lars tried to shield Beatrix from news of the war, but she was now seven years old and it was getting harder. Certainly there was no shielding her from the bombs, the crack of return antiaircraft fire by the Nazis, or the great searchlights that swept the sky in search of Allied planes.

There were hardly any nights now when sirens did not go off, when bombs didn't fall. Allied bombers were crossing Holland on their way to Germany, but there was no telling where they might unload their bombs. The week before, North Amsterdam had been badly bombed. Hundreds had been killed and many more taken to hospital.

Some families had built air raid shelters in their back gardens, but most, like Hans, Lars, and Beatrix, simply crawled under kitchen tables or staircases and held their breath as the bombs dropped. Only with the toot of the all-clear whistle did they emerge, tired and stiff, to begin their day.

Her plate clean, and not a crumb left, Beatrix sat at the large tin kitchen table and held a crayon in one hand while pinning down her drawing of a unicorn with the other. The girl unicorn was mostly yellow, with pink ears and a blue horn in the middle of her forehead. Holding the reins of the unicorn was a beautiful lady. The lady always held an apple.

"What is the lady's name?" Hans sometimes asked. Beatrix shook her head firmly. They knew it was Mamma, of course, but Hans and Lars did not press for more information. They believed that she would tell them when she was ready, when the war was over.

There was a knock at the door—a special knock. "Go let Mrs. Vos in," said Lars as he gathered up the coupon books. Beatrix hopped off the chair and ran down the hall. Normally Beatrix was not allowed to answer the door.

Mrs. Vos, wearing a nightcap and a coat over her nightgown, bade Beatrix a quick good morning as she hurried down the hall to the kitchen. Hans and Lars looked up in shock. Mrs. Vos was always very particular about her clothes.

"Lieve just stopped in on her way to the office. She says there has been an announcement. All Jews must assemble in the city square for deportation." Mrs. Vos was out of breath and pale. She did not look at all well.

"Please, sit down, Mrs. Vos," said Hans.

"Where?" She looked around the kitchen. Where indeed! All the chairs were stacked with books, or mending, or drawings.

"Uncle Lars, do I have to go to the square?" asked Beatrix as she picked up the blue crayon.

All three—Hans, Lars, and Mrs. Vos—stood very, very still. Lars bent down beside Beatrix. The tears in his eyes were sudden.

"They are going to the square to having a meeting, that is all. But remember, you are not Jewish. You are Catholic now," said Lars.

"Mamma told me that I was never to tell anyone I was Jewish."

"Good girl. Off you go and find your rain hat. It might rain today," said Hans.

Once Beatrix was out of earshot the three talked in hisses and whispers. It was rumored that the Nazis would track down Jews house to house if they had to. Special search teams had been formed to hunt down hidden Jews. "Neighbors, anyone, can earn as much as 7.50 guilders if they report a person hiding in their neighborhood," whispered Mrs. Vos. Hans and Lars nodded. It was not a rumor. They had read the notice. And 7.50 guilders was a lot of money—enough to feed them all for a week or more.

They listened to rumors. They made it their business to know as much as they could. And they were not as naive as they had once been about the war, about the ruthlessness of the Nazis. Everyone knew about Westerbork now. Jews, and any people the Nazis did not like, were herded into the camp to wait for the trains that would take them farther east to the work camps. There were stories that many died in those camps. Once they had thought such behavior impossible for civilized Europeans. Now they believed that the Nazis were capable of murdering anyone—even a child.

"Don't take her on the tram. Leave Beatrix with me," said Mrs. Vos.

Hans and Lars considered, pondered, discussed it, but in the end they thought, *What if they came for her during the day? How would an eighty-one-year-old woman protect the child?*

"But surely taking her on the tram is more dangerous," said Mrs. Vos.

"Hide in plain sight," said Hans.

Lars agreed. He wanted her close. "She is seven, but small for her age, and children under six are not required to carry identification," he said.

"Besides, she has never been asked for papers yet. And surely the Nazis have better things to do!" added Hans. No, for now they believed that the child was safest with them.

Beatrix came back into the kitchen wearing her rain hat. "I'm almost ready," she announced.

"We will talk about this tonight," said Mrs. Vos. She turned to Beatrix. "You be a good girl." And she kissed the little girl on the cheek. Beatrix smiled. Hans and Lars were astonished. In living memory neither had ever seen Mrs. Vos kiss anyone.

"Come now." Hans held up Beatrix's coat as Lars put the crayons away and tacked the unicorn up on the kitchen wall that was already covered with unicorns, dogs, horses, and of course trains, trams, and automobiles. There were other pictures, mostly drawings of menacing fire-breathing dragons.

Hans tried his best to clear the table but really what he did was make piles at one end. Under the crayon box he found a drawing of a man. He was tall and skinny, with brown hair. "Who is this?" Hans held up the picture.

"Papa, except I don't really remember what he looks like," said Beatrix.

"Why is your papa wearing a cross around his neck?" he asked.

Beatrix shrugged. She was not supposed to talk about her past, but wasn't it all right to make drawings of her family?

Hans pinned up the picture of Papa. Naturally there were pictures of Hans and Lars too. Hans thought that the drawing of him made him look fat. Lars assured him that it was a near-exact portrait. Lars thought that the drawing of him made him look too skinny. "Not at all," said Hans. "It could be a photograph."

"Where are your mittens? It's still cold out." Lars picked up a copy of Beatrix's storybook *De Zoom van Dik Trom* and peered underneath. He shifted the box of crayons, and ducked under the clothesline that had been strung up over the stove to dry wet leggings, mitts, and socks. There were dishes in the sink, but they could wait until tonight.

Mittens found, lunches and books packed, Hans stood in the doorway and looked up at the sky. It was a clear day, but still he reached for his umbrella.

"It's not going to rain or snow today, Uncle Hans." Beatrix giggled.

Both Hans and Lars sniffed the wind. "I think she is right, Lars," said Hans. Beatrix removed her hat and Hans and Lars left their umbrellas and rain boots behind. As was their habit, the three left the house and walked the six blocks to the tram depot.

CHAPTER 10

Beatrix sat in the seat on the tram behind Uncle Hans. She placed her paper-wrapped sandwich on the seat next to the window. Often she brought an apple, but not today. Uncle Lars's old school knapsack, filled with books, a pencil case, and lined paper, was on her other side.

Beatrix could read and write and knew her Catholic catechism. She liked the Fourth Commandment best, "Honor your father and your mother."

Lieve was a great teacher. She read poetry to Beatrix and taught her English too, but in secret. The Germans did not want people speaking English. *Hat, mitten, shoe, boot, glove, dress*—she knew lots of English words.

Hans and Lars read to her every night. She knew all about the combustion engine, the history of the automobile, and how to build a greenhouse. They had great plans to build a greenhouse at the back of the garden once the war was over. And Mrs. Vos had taught Beatrix to knit.

"*Goedemorgen*," said the nun, wishing the brothers a good morning, with a nod to Beatrix. Every once in a while, one of their regular passengers got on the tram.

"*Goedemorgen*," replied Beatrix.

The nun lumbered down the tram aisle and took her usual seat.

While Uncle Lars collected tickets and money from the passengers, and Uncle Hans made the tram go and stop, Beatrix kept an eye on her favorite passengers. There was the nice-looking older lady who occasionally smiled at her, the girls in school outfits, and the nun in her not-so-white–winged hat. The older boy who always sat right behind her wore a different uniform now. He didn't wear short pants any more. He was very tall now. He looked like a real soldier, and today he had a great big bag with him. Sometimes she smiled at him, but he never smiled back.

None of the regulars seemed to think it odd that a child rode the tram every day. Since the invasion, everything was odd. One woman who rode the tram three times a week had asked about Beatrix.

"She is our niece, an orphan," said Lars.

"Poor little thing. There are so many orphans wandering about with no place to go. She is a lucky girl to have a place to live." And that was the last time anyone had inquired about Beatrix riding the tram.

There were other people on the tram too, sometimes so many that she had to slide over and hold her belongings tight to her chest. The best times were when the tram was empty and Beatrix and Uncle Lars and Uncle Hans had it all to themselves. Uncle Hans would drive very slowly and Beatrix would help Uncle Lars polish the brass. The tram was her second home.

But today the tram was packed. The aisles were full too, and everyone seemed very grumpy.

"I'm telling you, it happened! My daughter-in-law works at the hospital. The special security police took them all in the middle of the night—just pulled them out of their beds. All Jews. Terrible. The doctor wanted to know where his patients were being taken. And do you know what they said to him? Camp Westerbork."

Lars stood beside the two unfamiliar passengers. He heard every word quite plainly. Why was the woman speaking in such a loud voice? It wasn't safe to talk like that in public. He glanced over at Beatrix. Did she hear as well?

Lars moved toward the back of the tram. "Tickets?" he called out.

A hand reached out, holding a ticket. The hand was thin, the fingers tapered—he recognized it. It belonged to the young woman disguised as an old woman. Today she was wearing a padded, baggy coat with three buttons, a scarf tied under her chin, and thick glasses. He felt a kind of relief. He suspected that she was part of what was called "the underground," ordinary Dutch people who fought bravely against the Nazis in secret. She had been riding the same tram, on and off, for two years now, always in the disguise of an old woman.

Lars knew the pattern. The young woman in disguise would board first. Then a man, or occasionally a woman, would board the tram several stops later. The men often looked wounded or sick. The woman would get off at the front of the tram and the man at the back. They would soon be lost in the crowds. Perhaps she helped these young men and women escape to England. Maybe she found them medical help. Whatever her job, he was happy to see that this woman was still safe.

Hans slammed on the brakes and the tram came to an abrupt halt. His head bobbed as he checked in the mirror to see that Beatrix was safe. Hans sighed. This was the third time this month that the tram had been boarded by Nazi soldiers.

It was always the same. Two soldiers boarded at the front of the tram, and one stood beside Hans while the other pushed his way down the aisle.

Lars positioned himself in front of the young woman in disguise. If she moved quickly, she could get off the back of the tram without being noticed.

The soldier came up to Lars and shoved him aside. "Get out of my way," he yelled. Lars stepped to one side and looked back. The young woman was gone.

A covered military truck pulled up alongside the tram.

"Papers?" The soldier at the front of the tram hovered over Beatrix like a bird of prey.

"Beatrix," Lars whispered under his breath.

Hans's hands shook. His heart had been giving him some trouble of late, but now a pain shot up his arm. He crouched over the controls. "Lars," he hissed. "LARS!"

Lars was struggling to weave his way through the passengers standing in the aisle. He was a few feet away from Beatrix when he heard, "She is with me. She is my sister."

Hans looked up into the driver's mirror. Lars also paused, between a large woman carrying a bag of potatoes and a grumpy-looking man wearing spectacles.

"I am dropping her off at school and then reporting to my regiment. I leave for the front today." The boy who had once worn the short pants of the Hitler Youth now stood in a Nazi uniform and stared down at the soldier.

The soldier's head swiveled back to Beatrix, then back to the soldier. There was a moment of silence, and then the soldier raised his hand in salute and shouted, "*Heil* Hitler." The young soldier returned the salute and thumped down on the seat.

Six people were taken off the tram, including two children. None were regulars, none put up a fight. Lars watched. Will the soldiers take these people to the camps? What happens in these camps? It was as if people were marched into a fog. No one came out of the fog, ever.

Stone-faced but breathing steadily, Hans inched the train forward. His heart returned to a steady rhythm and matched the *clickity-clack* of the tram as it glided over the tracks. Lars, as pale as a living man could be, went back to collecting tickets.

Beatrix picked up her books, her lunch wrappings, and her crayon box, and sat beside the young soldier. They rode in silence for two stops.

"Are you leaving Amsterdam?" Beatrix pointed to the large duffle bag at his feet.

A moment passed, then two. "I am German. We live here since Germany took control over your country. I go to the Russian front. My father SS. He believes it will make a man of me." He spoke in halting Dutch.

"Is it nice there?" Beatrix asked in all innocence.

The boy shrugged and then shook his head. "I think it is not nice and very cold."

Two stops later the young soldier stood and picked up his duffle bag.

Beatrix reached up and touched the cuff of his uniform. "*Geb achting*."

Lars stood a few feet away. He heard. Hans heard too. What did she say? Was it Yiddish? It was all Hans could do to keep his hands on the controls. Lars held on to the overhead bar, and Hans pulled up to the tram stop. People were standing on the tram, front and back, ready to disembark. Hans looked up into the mirror.

The boy in the uniform was bending over Beatrix. What was he doing? He was whispering something. Lars stopped. Hans waited. For both, it was as if they were suspended in time. The young soldier left the tram and melted into the crowd.

"Beatrix?" Lars tried to control his voice. A crowd piled onto the tram. They pushed past him. Beatrix looked up and smiled at Uncle Lars. Hans pushed down on the pedal and the tram lurched forward.

It was apparent to both Hans and Lars that Beatrix could no longer ride the tram every day. It was not safe.

"What is wrong?" Mrs. Vos flew into the kitchen.

Lieve was hot on her heels. "I got your note." She and Mrs. Vos had found little ways of communicating news. A scrap of paper pushed under the door that said "I have an extra potato" meant "We must meet soon." A scribble that read "Do drop by for tea" meant "Come immediately."

"What's happened?" Lieve looked from face to face.

Beatrix sat at the table clutching her hands. Tears rolled down her face. "I didn't mean to do anything wrong," she sobbed.

"Hush, sweetheart. Tell me what happened." Lieve wrapped her arms around Beatrix.

"She spoke Yiddish to a German soldier," said Lars as he put his hand on Beatrix's head and stroked her hair. Beatrix buried her head in Lieve's shoulder.

"Yiddish!" Mrs. Vos covered her mouth with her hand.

"No more tears. Beatrix, look at me. Tell me, what did you say to him?" Lieve was calm and her voice was low and controlled.

"I said what a lady said to Mamma once, '*Geb achting.*'"

"What does that mean, Beatrix?" said Lieve.

"I think it means to be careful. He said he was going to a cold place. He was nice to me." Beatrix burst into tears all over again.

"And what did he say in return?" asked Lieve.

"He whispered in English. He said, 'Do I got mittens?'"

Mrs. Vos, Lars, and Hans sat back, perplexed.

"Why would a young German soldier speak in English?" asked Mrs. Vos.

"Wait, I think I understand," said Lieve. "He was not speaking English. He was speaking German. Beatrix, did he say, '*Gott mit uns*'?" Beatrix nodded. Lieve sighed. "He said, 'God with us.'"

"What did he mean? Who is God with?" asked Hans. "Does he mean that God is with the Nazis, or that God is with us all? He is only a boy. Does he mean God is with children?" Four adults and one child sat in silence. No one had the answer.

"He got off the tram and walked away," said Hans.

"Beatrix, you were very lucky today. Listen carefully. You must not speak Yiddish again, not until the war is over. Understand?" said Lieve.

Beatrix nodded. "But I don't know any Yiddish, not really!" And she began to cry all over again.

Later, as Beatrix lay tucked up in the great brass bed, Hans, Lars, Lieve, and Mrs. Vos sat downstairs drinking weak tea. It was agreed that from now on Beatrix would stay with Mrs. Vos during the day.

"She would be safest in school, but she needs some sort of identity papers, a birth certificate, something!" Lieve, Hans, and Lars agreed.

"But we know of no one who might help," sighed Hans.

"I know someone," said Lars.

CHAPTER 11

Lars paced the aisle of the tram, his eyes peering out the windows, searching, searching. The day passed slowly. It felt as if every minute were an hour. And, finally, there she was! Hans looked up into his mirror and blinked. Lars nodded back. As Lars's knees knocked, Hans's heart thumped in his ears.

The woman boarded the tram and sat midway down on the left.

"Ticket?" whispered Lars.

The young woman, disguised as an old woman, as usual, handed Lars her ticket. Lars punched it and handed it back, along with a small bundle wrapped so tightly one would hardly notice that money, a note, and a photograph were being slipped from hand to hand. Startled, the woman looked up, but Lars had already turned to the next passenger.

"Ticket?" he asked.

She did not board the tram the next day, or the one after that. A week passed. The two brothers imagined all sorts of things. What if Lars had made a mistake? What if she was a spy who worked for the Nazis? What if … what if … ?

Two weeks later the woman boarded the tram, as usual. Again, Lars's heart thumped as he tried to draw in deep breaths. He took her ticket. She said nothing, nor did she look at him. She left the tram several stops later, as usual. Lars wanted to call out, to say something, but what could he say? And just when disappointment and fear were about to overwhelm him, he spotted a small envelope pushed into the wooden slats of the seat.

Later that evening, when Beatrix was tucked into bed, Lars, Hans, Lieve, and Mrs. Vos gathered around the table and looked at the identification papers. Her name was Beatrix Gorter. It was official: they were a family. And now Beatrix could go to school.

The primary school was on the tram line. Hans and Lars shook like leaves as they walked into the school building, but Beatrix held their hands tightly and assured them that it would be all right.

Her teacher's name was Mrs. Giest.

As Hans and Lars left the building, Mrs. Giest said to another teacher, "Wasn't it lucky that she had two uncles to take her in after her poor parents were killed in an air raid?"

CHAPTER 12

"Now, Beatrix, let's hear it," prompted Lieve. They had returned from church and now sat in Mrs. Vos's house enjoying a cup of watery tea and dry, sugarless biscuits. For Beatrix there was a special treat—orangeade.

Beatrix liked church. She liked the smell of incense and wax. Most of all she liked the funny hats the priests wore. In the beginning she had giggled a lot, but now it was all familiar and comforting. Uncle Lars always gave her a few coins to buy a candle. He never asked her who she lit the candle for, but he knew that it was for her mother.

"Come, Beatrix, you can do it," Lieve coaxed her in a gentle singsong voice.

Mostly Beatrix liked being with Lieve. It wasn't that she didn't love Uncle Hans and Uncle Lars, and Mrs. Vos too, but sometimes she could pretend that Lieve was Mamma. It was silly. Lieve was tall and blond and Mamma was tiny and dark. And they didn't sound alike either. But they were both gentle and kind, and they both hugged her the same way. It was a big, rocking hug, ending with a kiss on the top of her head.

Beatrix bounced off the chair, flattened her dress with her palms, and took a deep breath.

"I believe in God, the Father Almighty, maker of heaven and earth. And in Jesus Christ, His only Son, our Lord ..."

The words rolled off her tongue. On she went, without making a single mistake, right up to the ending, "*... and the life everlasting. Amen.*"

She curtsied as everyone applauded. Uncle Hans beamed, there were tears in Uncle Lars's eyes, and Mrs. Vos marveled at it all.

Religion was not terribly important to Hans and Lars. What was important was that Beatrix was safe. And if being a Catholic would keep Beatrix safe, then that was what she would be. They thought of her safety from morning till night.

"My girl!" Lieve threw open her arms as Beatrix fell into them. "Well done, my darling," Lieve whispered in her ear.

"You have taught her well, Lieve." Mrs. Vos gave a regal nod of approval. "Beatrix, fetch a few more biscuits from the tin in the kitchen, please."

Beatrix, still grinning from her performance, skipped toward the kitchen.

"And does she still cry for her mother at night?" Mrs. Vos fixed her sights on Hans and Lars, rather like a searchlight scanning the night sky for enemy planes.

Hans and Lars shook their heads, and Hans leaned forward and whispered, "No, but she still has nightmares." Lars nodded. Beatrix's cries woke them from the deepest sleep. They would rush into her room, sit at her bedside, and whisper, "Hush, hush. You are safe. We love you." She would nod off back to sleep and not remember a thing in the morning.

"And does she still sleep with that old train of yours?" asked Mrs. Vos.

"It is wrapped in a towel," said Hans, rather defensively.

"To make it soft," chimed in Lars.

"And she won't sleep without it," added Hans.

She pursed her lips and shook her head as Lieve laughed. "What she needs," announced Mrs. Vos, "is a doll."

Startled, Beatrix stopped in the threshold between parlor and kitchen, carrying a plate with the last few biscuits on it. She could not help but overhear. A doll? She almost lost her breath. She squeezed her eyes shut.

"Beatrix, what's wrong? You are as white as a sheet." Lieve stood up, her empty teacup in her hand.

Beatrix shook her head. She heard Mamma's voice: *Tell no one.*

Lieve put her teacup down and crossed the room to Beatrix, taking her back to the kitchen, where they could speak quietly. "Come, sit," she said. "Tell me."

"It's about the doll," whispered Beatrix.

"Do you not want a doll?" Lieve spoke gently, carefully, searching Beatrix's face for clues.

"I had a doll once," Beatrix said.

"What was the doll's name?" Lieve ran her hand over Beatrix's hair.

"Sophiia."

"I love that name. Sit beside me and tell me about Sophiia."

"I promised Mamma ..."

"Your Mamma wanted to keep you safe. You were younger then, and she was afraid that you might tell the wrong person something that could get you into trouble. But you are safe now, Beatrix. We love you. This is your home." Lieve pulled Beatrix in close. "Tell me about Sophiia."

"Mamma and I were living in a room on the top floor of a building. One night there was hammering on the door downstairs. We could hear the neighbors crying out. We heard, '*Aufmachen!*'—Mamma said it meant 'Open the door!'—and then there was shouting." Beatrix stopped and covered her ears with her hands.

"You are safe, Beatrix. What happened next?" Lieve gently pulled Beatrix's hands forward and held them in her own.

"The Nazis had come for everyone in the building. We were always afraid of that, so Mamma and I slept with our clothes on, every night, and we packed a little bag and left it by the door. We heard the soldiers coming up the stairs. They banged on the Livermans' door. We could hear their baby crying too. And over and over, at every door, we heard, '*Aufmachen,*' '*Aufmachen,*' '*Aufmachen.*'

"Mamma grabbed the bag, opened the window, and crawled out onto the fire escape. She said, 'Give me your hand, Beatrix.' I was so scared. Mamma took hold of my hand and I climbed out onto the fire escape too. We pressed our backs against the outside wall and looked down into an alley. It was dark, but we could see soldiers with big flashlights. The lights flashed on big, mean dogs. We could see the Livermans and the Goldbergs getting into army trucks. There were other families too. Then we heard soldiers in our room, right behind us. And that's when I remembered Sophiia," Beatrix cried. "I'd left her behind."

Beatrix rested her head on Lieve's shoulder, and for awhile it was enough to just rock back and forth.

"Come, we will make another pot of tea," said Lieve as she kissed Beatrix on the head.

In the parlor, the conversation about a doll continued. Hans and Lars looked at each other, then back at Mrs. Vos.

"Where would one get a doll?" Lars asked.

"Next Saturday afternoon, while Beatrix is having her lessons with Lieve, you will go to the shop and buy her one," said Mrs. Vos with her usual authority.

Hans and Lars nodded. They had learned many things over the past year. They knew how to braid hair (Lars was very good at it, although it took him many tries to get the braids even on the opposite sides). They could hem dresses, help with homework, and meet with teachers. They had attended school recitals and tea parties, skated on the canals in winter (Hans fell down), and gone on bicycle rides in summer (Lars fell off). Now they would go doll shopping. And, in fact, they wondered why it had not occurred to them to do it sooner.

CHAPTER 13

On Saturday morning Lars braided Beatrix's hair. Hans pressed her dress, although it was now terribly worn-out.

As soon as Beatrix had dressed and finished her breakfast, Hans held out her winter coat while she slipped it on, and then he plopped a bright red tam on her head. He had found it in the market, and Mrs. Vos had knitted her matching red mittens. Then Hans and Lars watched her skip down the road to Lieve's house.

Beatrix waved to Mr. Van Engle, who lived at number 3. The man scoffed and turned his back. She waved to Mrs. Jensen-Smit at number 6. Mrs. Jensen-Smit took hold of her son Pieter's hand and pulled him into the house. At the last possible second, just before the door closed, Pieter waved at Beatrix. And then he was gone.

"You're here!" Lieve flung open the door and gave Beatrix a big hug. "I have a surprise for you in the parlor and a treat in the kitchen. Which do you want first?"

Beatrix giggled, but she didn't have to choose because she looked over Lieve's shoulder and saw the most beautiful dress in the world spread out on the sofa. The neck was high and made of lace. It had slightly padded shoulders and a beautiful, swirly skirt with a sash!

"Is it for me?" Beatrix tiptoed toward it as if making a loud noise would shatter the dream.

"I used to make clothes for myself and my sisters. Do you see this neckline? It's called a *bobbit kraagje*. And see the shoulders? They are slightly padded so that it will look as though you have a very tiny waist—which you already have! My sisters loved fashion. Do you want to try it on?" asked Lieve.

Beatrix nodded her head so fast her braids jumped up and down. She hung up her coat on a special hook that was just the right height, and then peeled off her old dress. She stood in her bloomers and undershirt in the middle of the room.

"Hands up." Lieve pulled the dress over Beatrix's head. "Oh dear, it's too big in the waist and it's too long. But that is easily fixed. And I think I can take it in on the sides too. You are skin and bones, child," Lieve said. "The sash is silk. I dyed it blue. It's from my wedding dress."

"Your wedding dress?" Beatrix put her hand to her mouth.

"I think it's wonderful that my old dress can be turned into something new and pretty. Look, I'll tuck the silk flower to the sash. See? Now, I'll just pin up the waist and that will make the skirt flare out even more. You look like a princess!"

"It's the most beautiful dress in the world!" Beatrix twirled around and around. She stopped. There were tears in Lieve's eyes. "What's the matter?" Beatrix held her breath. When Mamma cried bad things happened.

"Nothing. I was just thinking about my little sister. You remind me of her." Lieve took a handkerchief from her sleeve and dabbed her eyes.

"Where is she now?" asked Beatrix.

"Both my sisters were killed at the beginning of the war." Lieve paused for a moment as if trying to compose herself.

"What were your sisters' names?" asked Beatrix.

"Margot and Lize," said Lieve.

"You miss them like I miss Mamma." Beatrix leaned her head on Lieve's shoulder.

"Yes, every day." Lieve kissed the top of Beatrix's head. "Let's not be sad. Why don't I help you out of the dress? You might get stuck by a pin. Then you can see what your treat is." Lieve stood and squared her shoulders.

"Please, can I keep it on for just a little longer? I'll be careful."

"Of course. It's yours now, or it soon will be once I make the alterations."

Beatrix threw her arms around Lieve's waist. "I am sorry about your sisters. I love you," she whispered.

"My dear girl, I love you too. Come, come get your treat. I used up all my sugar rations to make this." Lieve led the way to the kitchen.

There it was, on the kitchen table, just sitting there. A cake! And not just any cake but *kersttulband.*

"It's called a Christmas ring cake." Lieve clapped her hands and laughed.

Beatrix nodded. "Mamma used to make it for Papa," she whispered. "Your papa?" Lieve's smile dropped away. She stood still and stared at Beatrix.

"Papa was Christian," said Beatrix. She'd hardly known what the word meant, back when she was little and they were all together, but she did know that Papa celebrated Saint Nicholas Day, which was the best day in the whole year because everyone got presents.

"Christian!" Lieve could hardly get the word out.

Beatrix's head bobbed up and down. She could not take her eyes off the cake. It was round with a hole in the middle and sprinkled with white sugar. Oh, how she wanted a slice of the cake.

"Beatrix, what happened to your papa?" she asked gently.

"I don't remember, but Mamma said the Nazis took him. Then Mamma got a letter that said he was never coming home. They said he was a *compitist.*"

"A Communist?"

"Yes." Beatrix nodded. "Mamma said that he was a good man who loved his country. But now it's hard to remember him."

"Have you told Uncle Lars or Uncle Hans about this?" Lieve's voice kept catching.

"Mamma said that I must not talk to anyone about our past. I promised."

"Beatrix, you have to trust me. What about your grandparents? Where do they live? If they are Christian, perhaps they can help you." Still shocked, Lieve thumped down in a chair and pulled Beatrix close.

Beatrix shook her head, slowly at first and then faster and faster. Tears rimmed her eyes.

Lieve spoke softly. "Hush, try to tell me. What do you remember?"

Beatrix covered her ears. The joy of her new dress, of seeing the cake, flew away.

Lieve gently pulled Beatrix's hands down and held them in her own. "Tell me, please."

"We went to Opa's and Oma's house. It was dark. My legs were tired. I saw the house. I had been there before, but with Papa.

"Mamma went to Opa's back door and knocked. A dog barked and we got scared. I wanted him to open the door. I kept thinking, *Opa, open the door. Opa, open the door.* And then, there he was. I was so happy, but Opa was not happy. He looked like a dragon with fire in his nose. Then he shouted, but not so loud that anyone could hear. He said, 'Go away. You put us all in danger. Go away.'

"I hid behind Mamma. I could see Oma was standing behind Opa. She was crying and pulling at his clothes. She said, 'Johannes, no. Let them in.'

"Mamma was crying. She went down on her knees. I tried to pull her up. I told her that she would get all dirty. Mamma said, 'Just take Beatrix. I will go. Keep her safe.

She is your granddaughter.' I tried to tell Mamma that I didn't want to stay with a dragon. I kept saying, 'Get up, Mamma, get up.' Then the door closed." Beatrix buried her head in Lieve's shoulder. "They did not want me."

Lieve hugged her tight. "I want you. Uncle Hans and Uncle Lars want you. And Mrs. Vos too. We love you, Beatrix. We all love you."

CHAPTER 14

Hans and Lars stood in De Bijenkorf on Dam Square, Amsterdam's finest department store. The sheer size of it—six stories high and several blocks long—took their breath away. De Bijenkorf meant 'The Beehive,' and they did indeed feel like they were surrounded by busy, busy bees.

The two brothers stood on the ground floor in the luxury goods department and wondered what to do. Even though it was wartime, there were so many things for sale that they couldn't help feeling overwhelmed. They had lived in Amsterdam all their lives, but they had never been to the famous department store before. After all, when their mamma was alive she had bought them everything they needed. And now, with the war on, they had learned to make do with what they had or what they could buy at the local market.

"Lars, there is not a German soldier in sight," whispered Hans.

"That's because the owners are Jewish and the store is considered a 'Jewish concern,'" Lars whispered back. Much as they might have wanted to, not even the Nazis could shut down a store that was so near and dear to the hearts of the Dutch.

"May I help you?" a saleswoman asked. Lars jumped.

Being the elder, Hans took the lead. "We are here to buy a doll," he said.

"Ah, the toy department. The elevator is straight ahead. The elevator operator will direct you."

Up and up they went. And in no time they were surrounded by dolls. There were blond dolls wearing traditional Dutch costumes with white aprons and white caps. There were baby dolls, walking dolls, and dolls wearing frilly bloomers and fancy dresses. None of them seemed quite right. Hans and Lars dithered.

"May I help you?" asked another saleswoman.

"Yes," said Lars.

"No," said Hans.

Both were embarrassed into momentary silence.

"Yes," said Hans.

"No," said Lars.

Again, for a moment, no one spoke. And then, "We would like to buy a doll," said Lars.

"Yes, we want to buy a doll," said Hans.

Silence.

"Not for ourselves," added Lars.

"For our niece. It's a surprise," said Hans.

"What kind of child is she?" asked the saleswoman.

"She is this tall," said Hans as he raised his hand to his chest.

"And she has long, dark hair," added Lars.

Silence.

"How old is she?" asked the saleswoman.

"Seven," said Hans.

"Almost eight," added Lars.

Silence.

"Does she cry out in her sleep?" asked the saleswoman.

Both men cried in unison, "Yes!" Their shouts startled several shoppers.

"Ah, the war … She needs a doll to cuddle. This is the doll for your niece." The saleswoman chose a doll with light brown hair and brown eyes, dressed in pink.

Yes, that was the very doll that Beatrix would love, they were sure of it.

"She is expensive, ten guilders," the saleswoman added.

It was more money than they had ever spent on any one thing, but they nodded their heads in unison.

Hans handed the saleswoman a ten-guilder note. With a look bordering on smug, the saleswoman wrapped the doll in brown paper, tied the package up with string, and handed it to Hans.

They also bought Beatrix four hair ribbons. And just as they were about to leave the floor they spotted a child-sized nightgown. Should they? It had embroidery around the neck and sleeves and was much nicer than anything Hans could sew.

Yes, they should.

CHAPTER 15

The two older men walked along the sidewalk with a skip in their step. It had been the most enjoyable shopping day that either had ever had, and Hans was pleased to note that there was not even a hint of rain.

Hans carried the doll and Lars, the parcel containing the hair ribbons and nightgown. There were two embroidered hankies in the parcel too—one for Mrs. Vos and the other for Lieve.

"Look out!" Hans pulled his brother over to the curb.

A large Mercedes zoomed past them. These expensive cars were driven by the Nazi SS. A military truck covered in green and gray canvas followed close behind. Both vehicles were coming from the direction of their road.

Hans and Lars stood at the top of their cul-de-sac. At that moment, Mrs. Vos swung open her door and stumbled to her gate. "Hans, Lars, they took them!" Her face was stone gray.

Both men looked down the cobblestone road. Even from a distance they could see that Lieve's front gate and door were wide open.

"Beatrix!" Lars cried. They ran past Mrs. Vos. Lars was tall and long-limbed, but Hans's legs moved like wheels. The doll, the nightgown, the ribbons, the hankies slipped from their hands.

"Hans, Lars, wait!" Limping, her hand pressing down on her sore hip, Mrs. Vos did her best to catch up.

Hans and Lars reached Lieve's house at the same time, barged through the gate, and into the house.

"Beatrix?" Lars called out.

"Beatrix?" Hans chimed in. And then "Lieve, Lieve!" No answer.

Lars climbed the inside stairs, two at a time. Hans looked into the parlor, then ran into the kitchen. "Beatrix!" he cried. He twisted the knob on the door that led to the back garden. Locked.

The house was empty. Beatrix and Lieve were gone. A cake, smashed into crumbs, lay on the floor.

Lars thumped down hard on a stair and slumped forward, his head in his hands. "No, no, no. Please, God," he whispered. "Please."

Hans fell against the doorframe. A small sob escaped his lips as he spotted Beatrix's red tam on the floor. He reached for it, held it close, and bent his head over it. He hadn't cried since he was a boy, and now he could not stop.

Mrs. Vos stood in the doorway. "It happened so fast. That dreadful automobile, and then the truck … I came … I came … The soldiers called me a nosy old woman …" Mrs. Vos, her hand to her chest, huffed and puffed. Only then did they notice Mrs. Vos's dirty dress and her raw, scraped arms. Blood ran down from her knees and caked above her shoes. Her face was smudged.

"They hurt you." Lars came out of himself for a moment.

Mrs. Vos shook her head. "They pushed me down. I am all right."

"What did they want?" asked Hans.

"Perhaps there was an informer, but I believe that they were after Lieve. She said that her husband did 'war work.' I should have asked more questions. I should not have let Beatrix stay here." Mrs. Vos's voice cracked as she tried to draw in a breath. Grabbing the doorframe, she lurched into the house, fell into a chair, and covered her face with bruised hands.

"It is not your fault. It is war. There is no safe place," Hans whispered. Thoughts raced through Hans's mind—where would they take a child? Where could he go? What could he say? In the back of his mind was Westerbork, the prison camp.

"I should have asked Lieve more questions about her life, her husband. I should have …" sobbed Mrs. Vos.

"And what would she have said?" Lars shook his head. No one asked personal questions any more. It was dangerous to tell too much and dangerous to know too much. "Lieve would never have put Beatrix in danger. But if they wanted Lieve, why did they take Beatrix?" He rubbed his hand across his face. His hand was wet. Tears were sliding down his face.

Mrs. Vos shook her head.

"Did you see them take her?" whispered Hans. He was hunched in a corner. The strength in his legs, in his body, seemed to seep out of him.

"No, the truck—it was there." She pointed to the road. "And that big, awful car—it was in the way. I saw the top of Lieve's head, her blond hair. But I didn't see Beatrix." Mrs. Vos shook her head.

"You did not see them take her away?" Lars stood up.

"No, I told you. The truck ..."

Was it possible? Lars scrambled back up the stairs to check in closets and under beds.

Hans jumped up and kicked open the back door in the kitchen and ran around the little garden. He looked in the privy. He peered into the shed. "Beatrix, are you here?" He opened the coal bin. "Beatrix, come out." He looked to the end of the garden. "Lars, the gate—it's open," Hans bellowed. He didn't care who heard. Nothing mattered now, nothing.

Hans ran through the gate and down the lane. He passed behind number 6, number 4, and came to their own back gate. "Beatrix?" he cried.

He heard whimpering, kitten-like. Hans stopped. The sound was coming from behind the dustbins. With more strength than he'd ever thought he had, Hans picked up two huge bins and tossed them aside as if they were made of feathers. And there she was, huddled into a little ball.

"Dear girl, dear girl ..." Hans thought he might burst with relief. He reached out, picked her up, and held her.

"They took her, Uncle Hans. We heard the trucks coming. She told me to run. She pushed me out the back door and locked it tight." Beatrix gulped air. "They took her away. They took Lieve away. They took away my mamma. Why? Why? I want my mamma!" Beatrix raised her fists and pounded her Uncle Hans's chest.

The harder she pounded, the tighter he held her. "I have you. We love you. I have you. We love you," he whispered in her ear, over and over.

Soon Uncle Lars's arms were around them both, and Mrs. Vos's too. Tears streamed down the old faces.

"My dress is dirty." Exhausted, Beatrix rested against Uncle Lars. "Lieve made it for me."

"Lieve. We have lost Lieve," sobbed Mrs. Vos.

CHAPTER 16

Mrs. Vos, Hans, and Lars sat in a semicircle around the poor fire holding cups of watery tea, although in truth it was just hot water with a tea leaf floating on the top. Beatrix took her usual spot on the rag rug. They all wore coats.

They seldom talked about where Lieve might be. Mrs. Vos had made many trips to Gestapo headquarters, trying to get information. After her fifth trip, a young Dutch man who was working there approached her. "Do not come again. Your friend has been sent east." He may have been a collaborator—people who betrayed their own country by working with the Nazis—but perhaps he secretly worked for the Dutch underground. It was hard to tell. But if Lieve had been "sent east," it meant that she had been sent to the prison camps.

Beatrix had outgrown most of her clothes, despite Hans's efforts to lower hems and redo seams. Beatrix's special dress, the one made by Lieve, hung in the cupboard. She looked at it every day, touched it and sometimes hugged it, but wearing it was too hard.

Clothes were hard to find, and boots too. Lars discovered a pair of boy's brown corduroy pants in the attic. Hans altered the length for Beatrix. A belt and a pair of old suspenders helped keep them up. Mrs. Vos unraveled a wool blanket and knitted Beatrix a sweater. Hans nailed rubber from an old bicycle tire to the bottom of her worn-out boots. They made do.

Through the hard winter, though they were seldom paid, Hans and Lars never missed a day of work. Caring for a growing child was difficult on reduced wages, but everyone was in the same position, everyone was doing their best.

There were fewer and fewer private automobiles on the roads. Gas was rationed. Private cars were most often driven by Nazis or Dutch collaborators.

Everyone in Amsterdam was nervous. Hans said he could always tell if there were Nazis around the corner just by looking at the drivers in the oncoming traffic and noticing the way the pedestrians walked along the sidewalks. Were the faces of the drivers or pedestrians coming toward him flour-white? Were their hands gripping the wheel or clutching their packages? Were the pedestrians walking too quickly, with heads down as if charging into a stiff wind?

Hans and Lars had agreed to a routine. If Hans thought their tram was about to be boarded and searched, he would stop it before it reached the corner, get out, and with his hands on his hips examine the condition of the tracks. No one thought it was odd that a tram driver would peer down at the tracks, because the wooden blocks that held up the iron rails were often stolen. Pitched into the fireplace at home, the blocks would give off heat for an hour or more. Who could blame someone for stealing them? Everyone was cold.

As Hans stood looking down at the tracks at the front of the tram, Lars would swing open the back door and say, "We will be delayed. If anyone would prefer to walk, now is your chance." Over the past year the words *now is your chance* had become code for *Get off the tram, trouble ahead.*

In their own small way, Hans and Lars were doing their bit to fight the Nazis.

CHAPTER 17

1944
Amsterdam, The Hunger Winter

That winter there was a railway strike. The Dutch government, in exile in London, had asked Dutch railway workers to go into hiding, leaving no one to operate the trains. They were hoping that this would slow down the German army's transport of food and supplies for their troops. Then maybe the Allies, who had already liberated the southern part of the country, would be able to reach the rest of Holland as well. But the Germans retaliated by cutting off the supply of food from the farms to the city. Money did not matter. There was no food for the people of Amsterdam to buy at any price.

And then, in October, the city's tram service had to stop because there was not enough coal. Hans and Lars, for the first time in their adult lives, did not go to work.

Beatrix pulled a chair up to the window, pushed back the blackout curtains, and pressed her face against the window. Her breath made foggy circles on the glass. She drew faces in the circles: Hans, Lars, Mrs. Vos, Lieve, Mamma. If only she could remember what Papa looked like.

It was six o'clock, two hours away from curfew. Uncle Lars had left on his old bicycle at dawn with two blankets, two pairs of mittens, and three newly knitted wool hats in his basket. The wool had come from an old sweater that Mrs. Vos and Beatrix had carefully unraveled. Uncle Lars was going to the country to see if he could exchange the blankets and woolly things for food—butter, bread—and maybe a sliver of soap. Getting the food was hard. Getting past the Nazis on the way back was even harder. Nazi soldiers would stop anyone waking or pedaling and demand to see papers. Then the soldiers would steal the food, and sometimes the bike too.

Beatrix pressed her cheek against the glass and looked to the street corner. Where was he? She squeezed her eyes shut, counted to ten, and then opened them again. *Please, please, please, Uncle Lars, be there.*

"Beatrix, come away from the window." Mrs. Vos sat beside the coal hearth, long since gone cold, and tried to knit in the dark. Her fingers were swollen, and every stitch seemed to take a whole minute.

"There's no sense worrying, my girl," said Mrs. Vos. "It will take him awhile. You know that the rubber on his bicycle tires is worn down." Mrs. Vos spoke gently but her eyebrows were all bunched up and her mouth was pursed. Clearly she was worried too. Ever since she had closed up her house and moved in with them, Mrs. Vos had become a quieter, gentler person. Beatrix didn't like it. She wanted the old, bossy Mrs. Vos back. But living together was a good idea. They saved on fuel, and they shared what little food they could buy, trade, or scavenge.

Hans and Lars had set up four small camp beds in the sitting room. The beds formed a circle around an oil lamp. And when the oil had run out they'd used Mrs. Vos's wedding candles, and when the candles had burned down to nubs Lars had broken up bits of old furniture that had been stored in the shed and put that in the fireplace. Eventually the shed itself had gone up in smoke. The entire city was freezing. Trees had been chopped down in city parks, and if a house was left unattended, the doors, shutters, and windows were often ripped away.

"If you pull the blackout curtains, I could read to you. I have one candle left," said Mrs. Vos. She had found some old books in her attic, folktales mostly. "We could read *The Story of Sinterklaas en Zwarte Piet.* Isn't it nice to think about Saint Nicholas and Black Peter bringing presents on December the 5th? Perhaps this year he will bring you something nice to eat!"

Beatrix nodded, but the only present she wanted was for Uncle Lars to come home right now. Just as Beatrix was about to reach for a book, she saw him through the window.

"There he is!" She jumped off the chair.

"Careful, now. Don't fall," said Mrs. Vos.

Hans came down the stairs at the very same time.

"He's here! He's here!" Beatrix ran to the front door and flung it open. "You're home!" she cried.

Lars leaned his bike against the fence and extended his arms.

"Everyone was so worried, but I wasn't. I knew that you would be all right." She buried her face in his coat collar.

"What's this? Are you crying?" Lars lifted Beatrix's chin and looked into her watery eyes.

"No I'm not. I'm too big to cry, and anyway, I told you that I wasn't worried."

"Yes, you did tell me. It was my mistake." Lars kissed her on the top of her head.

Mrs. Vos joined the welcoming committee. "Come, dear girl, let your uncle get by. The blackout curtain is open. We don't want to get in trouble."

Wearily Lars wheeled the bicycle right into the house.

Lars was tired. It was not uncommon for him to bike thirty kilometers and return with two potatoes and a few tulip bulbs, but today his basket was full.

"Good, good. The soldiers did not stop you." Hans reached into the basket.

"Careful, Hans, there are three eggs wrapped up in cloth," said Lars.

"Three eggs!" Beatrix cheered, and under her breath she whispered, "Thank you, *Sinterklaas*."

There were also two potatoes, a pat of butter, a loaf of bread, and an onion—more food than they had seen all together in a month.

Hans reached into the bottom of the basket and pulled out a wooden block. He turned it over in his hand, then looked at his brother. For a moment there was quiet. They all knew where the block came from—the tram line. Without them, the trams could not run, but there was no coal to run the trams in the first place, and the block of wood would keep them warm. Hans took the bounty and whisked it off to the kitchen.

"Did you see anything? Is there any news?" Beatrix was back to her happy self and bounced around Lars like a puppy.

"I must sit," he said in a froggy voice. With his old coat still wrapped around him, and his wool hat pushed to the back of his head, Lars sat.

Hans returned with a cup of milk and chicory, a substitute for real coffee, and handed it to his brother. "Tell us," he said.

"I went to your nephew's farm." Lars nodded to Mrs. Vos, who in turn beamed. The farm belonged to her sister's son. They had been very generous with their food these last few months. "They have a radio. I listened to the BBC and Radio Oranje," said Lars. All three took a breath. It was a daring thing to listen to the British newscasts. "There is a new Dutch army."

"Will they liberate us?" Beatrix sat on the arm of the chair and leaned her head on Uncle Lars's shoulder.

"Yes, they will come with the Allied soldiers, you will see. It will be all right."

"Your hands are all cracked, Uncle Lars." Beatrix placed her small hand on his big hand.

"I am fine, dear girl." He smiled. He was happy and in this moment, content. It was a feeling that did not come often, and he knew would not last.

"Lars, how is it out there?" Mrs. Vos leaned in. She had not left the house in months. The effort was more than she could bear.

Lars shook his head and looked at Beatrix. Certainly he would not tell her that there were people begging and dying of starvation in the street—children too. He had never believed he would see starving people lying in the streets of Amsterdam. The little food that was produced on Dutch farms was taken by the Nazis and sent to Germany. Lars, a peaceful man, had never felt such anger, such hatred.

"There are many Dutch men and boys in hiding," he said.

"Why, Uncle Lars? Are they Jews too?" asked Beatrix.

Lars looked down at his worn-out shoes. What to say? "The Nazis are catching every man they can find between the ages of sixteen and forty-five and sending them east to work in the German factories. They are running out of men, just as they did in the last war."

After a feast of scrambled eggs and a slice of bread, the four of them lay in the parlor in the dark on the old, uncomfortable cots. They listened to the Allied planes flying overhead, on their way to Germany.

"That one is a Lancaster," whispered Beatrix. The air raids were so frequent now—sometimes three or four a week—that they had all learned to recognize the sounds each plane made. In the beginning there had been the British Bristol Blenheim. It was light, slow, and easily shot down by the German antiaircraft guns. The German Messerschmitts screamed, the British Lancasters droned, the German antiaircraft guns went *rat-tat-tat*. But falling planes shot out of the sky all made the same hollow whistle that ended in a thud.

A bomb landed nearby. The ground vibrated. Bits of plaster fell from the ceiling.

"Uncle Lars?" Beatrix cried out as she sat up in her cot. It had happened before, many times, but still it was hard to catch her breath, hard not to cry out. Should they stand in the doorway or duck under the table?

"It will be all right, dear girl. You will see. It will all be all right."

And finally they would hear the whistle blast that meant "all clear."

"Why won't the Allied soldiers cross the Rivers Rhine and Maas?" asked Beatrix.

Southern Holland had been liberated months ago, but the Allies had been unable to capture a key bridge that would have allowed them to move farther north. Lars shook his head sadly. If the war was not won soon, they would all starve to death.

Beatrix, Lars, and Mrs. Vos sat around the kitchen table while Hans stood over the stove. He had skinned three tulip bulbs the night before, removed the poisonous centers, then left them to dry overnight. Now he was baking them.

Hunger made their throats raw. It was hard to swallow. They sat quietly at the table and waited for a serving of baked tulip bulbs. Hans mashed the bulbs into a pulp, then mixed in water and the last pinch of salt they had in the house. He served a spoonful onto each plate. Even baked, the bulbs tasted woody, like sawdust.

"Try, Beatrix," Lars coaxed.

Beatrix nodded. Sometimes it was hard to sit up straight. Mostly Beatrix wanted to sleep.

"Wash it down with hot water, Beatrix." Mrs. Vos poured boiled water into a cup. They were out of tea leaves, the horrible ersatz coffee, and chicory too.

There was a hammering at the door! A tremendous pounding that set the ceiling fixtures swaying.

"The Nazis! Hide, Beatrix," cried Mrs. Vos, who was nearly deaf.

"No, listen," said Lars. The four sat very still and listened to the words that were shouted from the street. "The Canadians are here."

"What is that noise?" said Mrs. Vos.

"Canadians? I hear the word *Canadians*," said Hans.

The four crept across the kitchen and down the hall.

"Get back, Beatrix," Mrs. Vos cried out. "Wait, Hans. Don't open the door. Look out the window. Maybe it is a trick!" It was too late, the door was wide open.

Slowly Hans, Lars, Mrs. Vos, and Beatrix emerged from their little house and stood behind their gate. It was May 5, 1945. After five years of war, was it possible? Liberation? Mrs. Vos reached for Beatrix and pulled her close.

"Look, Uncle Hans!" Beatrix pointed to the tricolor red, white, and blue Dutch flags flying from rooftops.

"It's over," said Beatrix. And to herself she whispered, "Mamma, come home now. I am here."

"Wait here!" cried Lars. With the boundless energy of a young man, he bolted back into the house and up the stairs only to return with a rolled-up flag.

"Get the ladder. We will hang it from the roof!" cried Lars.

Hans chuckled. It was a startling sound. "What ladder?" They had chopped up the ladder for firewood months ago. "We will pin it up over the door," he said.

Hans ducked into the house for a chair, a small hammer, and nails. Lars stood up on the chair.

"You be careful, Lars. Don't fall," cried Mrs. Vos. Tired and hungry, she could still manage a good bellow when the occasion called for it.

"Mrs. Vos, the Nazis didn't get us. Hunger didn't kill us. I expect my brother can survive a climb on a chair."

Hans was laughing now. When was the last time any of them had laughed?

"Listen," said Beatrix. The cheers from the street at the top of the road, the roar of tanks and motorcycles and vehicles of all kinds, were getting louder and louder.

"Let's go see!" Beatrix pulled at Hans's hand.

"Wait, wait!" Mrs. Vos flew back into the house to change into her best dress.

Beatrix looked down at her old corduroy boy's pants. If only … And then she remembered Lieve's dress. Would it fit? She was taller but, like everyone in Amsterdam, skinny. Beatrix dashed up the stairs and pulled the dress out of her closet. She slipped it over her head and did up the sash. It had never been altered and now it did fit, perfectly.

"You look like a princess, my dear," said Uncle Hans as Beatrix came down the stairs.

"Lieve said that too." Beatrix held out the pretty flared skirt and swallowed the great big lump in her throat.

"Ohhh," was all the three could say when Mrs. Vos emerged. Small to begin with, Mrs. Vos had shrunk. Her best dress was pink, worn through, and now at least two sizes too big. But she looked so happy, years younger, it was as if the dress had worked some magic on her.

"You look lovely," said Hans as he offered her his arm.

They walked to the end of the road. Where had everyone come from? It was a parade. The street was full of soldiers, marching or driving tanks and trucks and jeeps. People—young women and boys mostly—had scrambled up onto tanks and they were cheering and waving. There were even drums and out-of-tune instruments playing wild music. Soldiers, with guns hung carelessly on their shoulders, waved and grinned. They threw packages into the crowd—chocolate bars and cigarettes. Young women ran out into the streets and tucked flowers into the soldiers' jackets.

"Are they the Canadians?" asked Beatrix.

"Yes," said Lars.

Beatrix stood between the two men. They held her hands tightly in their own. These were still dangerous times.

Beatrix pulled at Uncle Hans's sleeve. As he bent down, she stood on her toes and whispered, "The soldiers are huge and they all have big, white teeth."

The words were no sooner out of her mouth than one of the giants came directly toward them. He was tall, taller than anyone Beatrix had ever known, and he had red hair.

"How ya doing, kid? Like a chocolate bar?" He spoke in English. What could she say?

Uncle Hans answered for her. "We would be most honored to accept your gift and welcome you to our country. Thank you. Thank you." He spoke English! Beatrix looked up at her uncle with pride. He was so clever.

Tears fell from Hans's eyes. Uncle Lars was crying too, and so was Mrs. Vos.

"And these are for you, pretty lady." The soldier handed Mrs. Vos a chocolate bar too. Two chocolate bars! Mrs. Vos went as pink as her dress.

"Maybe these will come in handy." The soldier reached into his knapsack and pulled out two tins of meat and a pair of silk stockings. He handed them to Hans. "Have a good day!" said the soldier as he disappeared into a sea of khaki uniforms.

Hans tucked the tins deep into his pockets. These tins were more precious than diamonds.

Lars took the silk stockings and let them hang from his fingertip. "What good are these? They will not keep anyone warm."

"Goodness me!" said Mrs. Vos, and Beatrix giggled.

"We might trade them for food," suggested Hans.

"No!" Beatrix spoke louder than she'd meant to.

"What is it, Beatrix?" Mrs. Vos asked, but in her gentle voice.

"We can keep them for Lieve or Mamma … when they come back." The war was over. Mamma and Lieve could come home now.

Lars rolled the stockings, pressed them flat, and tucked them into his pocket. "When we get home you can put them in your drawer and keep them safe," he said.

CHAPTER 18

1945
Amsterdam, Spring

"Oh please, Uncle Hans, please, please, Uncle Lars! Can't we go out too?"

The celebrations in Amsterdam went on for days and nights. But Hans and Lars were adamant. The streets were not safe for a young girl like Beatrix, and so they celebrated in their little house with Mrs. Vos.

Tinned food was passed out freely, and while they all craved fresh bread, eggs, and vegetables, they were no longer hungry. Chocolate was a special treat to be savored with a cup of real coffee, and for Beatrix, cocoa.

The trams started up again a few weeks later. Beatrix took up her old familiar seat behind Uncle Hans as he drove the tram through the streets of the newly liberated city. Uncle Lars collected tickets.

The push and pull, the lurching and pitching of the tram, the sound of the brakes scraping on the rails were as familiar as birdsong. Never mind the sandbags, the rubble, the shabby buildings, everything was beautiful. The apple trees were in blossom, the air smelled sweet, and if Beatrix thought of her mother, she did not mention it out loud.

Lars stood at the top of the tram and looked down the aisle. He had not seen the nun for months. The young woman who wore the disguise of an older woman had vanished a year ago. What of the young boy wearing the Nazi uniform, the one who had saved Beatrix from capture? Where was he? What of all the young lives lost? There were so many who had taken the tram during those horrible years. What had become of them all?

Worse, photographs of the Nazi death camps in Poland and Germany— indeed, all over Europe—were in the papers. Some said that there were hundreds of such camps, maybe even thousands. But the information was confusing, and so hard to comprehend, and yet they did believe it. What to do? How to tell Beatrix that it was unlikely that her mother had survived?

Hans and Lars agreed to register Beatrix with the Red Cross on their next day off. The Red Cross was taking names and trying to reconnect family members, to find survivors. But would that give Beatrix false hope? Would it only lead to more disappointment?

"Let us try to keep this away from her until we know more," Mrs. Vos had said just last evening as they sat around a warm fire.

Lars looked at Beatrix sitting in the seat behind Hans. Once, he would have done anything in the world just to keep her alive. Now, he would do anything to keep her from getting hurt.

Beatrix opened her book by Mr. Hans Christian Andersen, and soon got lost in antics of Kai, Gerda, and the Snow Queen.

Lars saw the woman first. She boarded the tram at the rear and sat at the back. She wore an old, oversized coat. The soles of her shoes were almost worn through. She looked out the window and rubbed her hands together as if trying to rid them of imaginary dirt. Lars watched. There were many such people who roamed the streets of Amsterdam now. They all had the same look about them—gaunt, glassy-eyed, tortured. They walked carefully, as if the ground under foot were made of glass.

Lars walked down the aisle toward her. As he grew closer his chest tightened. He grabbed hold of the pole and steadied himself. He took another step, then another, until he stood over the woman.

"Ticket?" he asked.

She looked up. He knew those eyes. He had been looking into those eyes for three years.

"I am sorry, I have no money," she whispered.

"You may ride for free," said Lars.

Lars was thinking quickly. *Could it be?* This made sense to him. She would have registered her name with the Red Cross, and then gone to the place where she had last seen her daughter. That's what he would have done.

Lars looked toward the front of the tram. Beatrix was bent over her book.

The woman followed his eyes. She gasped. Slowly she stood and walked past Lars. She moved ahead, one step at a time, one seat at a time, her hands gripping the seat rails, her eyes fixed on the back of the head of a dark-haired child at the front of the tram. Lars walked behind, his arms extended. He thought she might faint.

Hans looked up into the mirror and caught Lars's eyes. With a nod, Lars pointed at the woman. Perplexed, Hans looked at her in the mirror. He had never laid eyes on her before, but there was no denying the resemblance. And maybe there was something else too, something he felt in his heart.

The tram was almost empty. An old man in the back was asleep. A young couple, still heady from all the festivities, had eyes only for each other.

The woman moved up again, until she sat across the aisle from Beatrix.

Beatrix turned her head and fixed her eyes on the woman. There was no hint of surprise, no grand gesture, no screaming—instead there was expectation and radiance. Beatrix reached out and touched the woman's face.

"I knew you would come back."

Mamma opened her arms and Beatrix fell into them.

Her name was Judith. That night Beatrix and her mother, Judith, slept together in the old brass bed.

A few days later, Hans and Lars fixed up their old playroom at the top of the house under the eaves. This became Beatrix's bedroom until she left for university. Judith took over their mother's old room, and as the weeks turned to months, and the months to years, she made it her own.

It would be many years before she would tell her daughter about life in hiding, about months with the resistance, her capture, about the transit camp Westerbork, and finally the train that took her to the death camp in Poland—Auschwitz. In the beginning, and for a long time, all she would say was that she felt blessed that her daughter was alive and loved.

Hans and Lars retired soon after the war. As they had once cared for her daughter, Judith now cared for them. She found happiness in keeping a home, tending a garden, and watching her daughter grow. She served their favorite foods. On Christmas Judith baked a Christmas ring cake and on Hanukkah they lit candles. There was always a bowl of apples on the table. In time, Judith found a kind of peace.

Mrs. Vos returned to her home across the street a few days after the Allied soldiers entered Amsterdam. Too old to cook her own meals, she joined Hans, Lars, Beatrix, and Judith for dinner every evening.

"Call me Abigail," Mrs. Vos said to Judith one evening. Lars's and Hans's eyebrows shot up. A similar invitation had never been extended to them.

When the crossing between houses became too difficult, Judith brought Mrs. Vos her meals and sat with her while she ate.

"I am tired, Judith," said Mrs. Vos. Her once powerful voice, full of authority and assuredness, was greatly diminished. "My sister's son and his wife were killed during the last days of the war. I believe my sister died of heartbreak. They were very kind to us during those last few months when we were so hungry. They had a farm, you see. Now I am the last of my family. I have just you, Hans, Lars, and that beautiful child. And if it were not for your girl, I would not have found my purpose. And what is life without purpose?" Mrs. Vos sighed. "Have I told you the story of how Lars nearly ruined Beatrix's hair? She looked as if she had been electrocuted."

"Yes, I heard," said Judith as she adjusted Abigail's blankets.

"And that they gave her a train engine to sleep with?"

"The train is on her dresser. I don't think she would part with it for the world." Judith picked up the dinner tray.

"Who told you all this?" Mrs. Vos lifted her hooded eyes and peered at Judith, although in truth she was now mostly blind.

"You did." Judith kissed Mrs. Vos's cheek. It was paper-thin and as soft as powder.

On a spring day, when Hans and Lars were out on their daily walk and Beatrix was at school, Mrs. Vos died in her armchair in front of the window. No one guessed that Mrs. Vos was a relatively well-off woman. She had inherited a great deal from her long-dead husband, and her frugal living and careful investments had resulted in her leaving behind a considerable sum. Mrs. Vos's estate was left to Beatrix on the condition that it was to be devoted first to Beatrix's education.

Beatrix discovered that her father's parents, Oma and Opa, the grandparents who had turned her and her mother away on that terrifying night, died when a bomb hit their home three days before liberation.

With the help of her mother, Beatrix investigated Lieve's arrest and abduction by the Nazis. Lieve van der Meer was held at Gestapo headquarters in Amsterdam for ten days. She was not charged with any crime, although it was recorded that her husband had escaped Holland and joined the British Royal Air Force. He flew a Bristol Type 156 Beaufighter, often referred to as "The Beau." He was shot down over Berlin. He did not survive. It was hardest of all to learn about what happened to Lieve. She was transported from Gestapo headquarters to Westerbork

Transit Camp in the northeastern Netherlands. From there she was sent to Bergen-Belsen, a death camp in northwestern Germany. She died on March 6, 1945. The camp was liberated on April 15, 1945, by the British.

While Beatrix eventually resumed her life as a Jewish girl and attended synagogue, she never failed to go into the Basilica of St. Nicholas every Saint Nicholas Day, on December 6, and light a candle in Lieve's memory.

CHAPTER 19

1960
Amsterdam, Summer

On a summer's evening, while sitting in the yard that Judith had transformed into a garden, Lars gazed over at their greenhouse, at its flowering blossoms that danced against the windows, and wondered at it all. He looked at Beatrix too. What a beauty she had become.

As usual, her head was bent over a book. She had just graduated from university and was engaged to a nice young man who lived in England. They had met at school, but which school? It was getting harder and harder for Lars to remember names. As he concentrated, little rivers formed across his brow and his mouth pulled in as tight as a drawstring purse. *Shoes. It is the same as a type of shoes, hmmm. Oxford, that's it! Beatrix went to Oxford University in England. But she mentioned a college too. What was its name? He pondered and then there it was, St. Hilda's!* He chuckled to himself.

"Why are you laughing, Uncle Lars?" Beatrix looked up from her book.

"I was thinking that I cannot imagine our lives without you in it," Lars said shyly as he glanced at the lovely young woman sitting a few feet away.

Beatrix closed her book, jumped up, and hugged him. "I love you bunches, you silly old uncle." She kissed him on both cheeks. Tears filled his eyes.

"Uncle Hans, careful!" cried Beatrix. Uncle Hans was walking down the garden steps without his cane. "Here, take my arm." Beatrix ran to his side.

They walked slowly to his special chair. Soon Judith would call them in for dinner. It was Friday, and so they would eat roast chicken, their favorite.

Hans and Lars died in 1961 within a week of each other, Lars in his sleep and Hans in his chair in the garden. Neither experienced any pain. All that they owned was left to Judith and Beatrix.

CHAPTER 20

1973
Amsterdam, Spring

The woman wore a trim pink suit. A matching pillbox hat sat on dark brown hair that curled up at her shoulders. She was thin, but not unnaturally so, graceful, and so stunning that heads turned as she walked. Perhaps, they thought, she was a dancer, or a fashion model?

She stood beside a child nine or ten years old. The child too was beautiful. She had a pixie look, a pointy but not sharp chin, wide, dark eyes, and a cap of black hair that peeked out under a felt hat. She wore a blue spring coat, white knee socks, black patent-leather shoes, and white gloves.

Mother and daughter stood at a tram stop.

"Mummy, are we going to meet Daddy for lunch?" The child spoke with a British accent.

"Yes, Lieve. Daddy knows where we are. He will wait. We are going to take a ride. I want to tell you a story." Beatrix looked up and down the busy road. A tram came to a squeaky stop right in front of them. "Up you get. Take the seat behind the driver."

Lieve climbed up the steps and turned back. "Where are we going, Mummy?"

"To the end of the line, my love."

AFTERWORD

Until World War II, the Dutch had not been in a war since 1830. The Netherlands had a strict policy of neutrality and did not fight in World War I. On 10 May, 1940, German troops invaded the Netherlands without a declaration of war.

The Nazis had about 750,000 soldiers, three times the Dutch army, and 1,100 planes. The Dutch had 125 planes, 6 armored trains, and 1 tank. And yet, the Germans lost over 500 planes during the five-day attack.

Hitler considered the Dutch people—excluding the country's Jewish population—to be almost 100 percent Aryan. Hitler's goal was to make the Netherlands part of Germany following the war. With this goal in mind, and with the exception of the bombing of Rotterdam, the conquering of the Netherlands was accomplished with a minimum of destruction. German soldiers were ordered to be nice to the citizens, and to pay top dollar for food, lodging, and consumer goods.

Amsterdam, the country's largest city, had a Jewish population of less than 80,000, which represented less than 10 percent of the city's total population. On February 22, 1941, the Germans arrested several hundred Jews. Dutch Jews were typically sent to the Westerbork Transit Camp and from there, starting in July 1942, they were deported to extermination camps such as Buchenwald, Mauthausen, Bergen-Belsen, and Auschwitz. Many city officials, including the Dutch police, Dutch railway workers, and the Dutch Nazi Party, cooperated in the deportation of Jews to camps.

An estimated 25,000 Jews, including 4,500 children, went into hiding to evade arrest. One-third were discovered and deported. In all, at least 80 percent of the Dutch Jewish community was murdered.

In May 1945, the Canadian Forces liberated Amsterdam.

Who is on which side?

The Allied Forces, led by Britain, were the armies that fought against the Nazis. The Allied Forces were composed of the United Kingdom (England, Northern Ireland, Scotland, and Wales), the British Commonwealth (Australia, Canada, Newfoundland, New Zealand, South Africa, and India), the Union of Soviet Socialist Republics, Denmark, France, and Yugoslavia. Other Allies included Belgium, Brazil, Czechoslovakia, Ethiopia, Greece, Mexico, the Netherlands, Norway, and Poland. The United States of America joined the war effort on December 8, 1941, after the bombing of Pearl Harbor. It declared war on its attacker, Japan. Germany and Italy declared war on the United States on December 11, 1941, bringing the United States into the European war.

The Axis powers were made up of Germany, Austria, Italy, and Japan.

Into the arms of strangers

With the rise of the Nazi Party in Germany, the persecution of the Jewish population began. Even before the outbreak of World War II, as the violence escalated, it was clear to many families that the only way to keep their children safe was to send them away. And so a program called Kindertransport was created. In this rescue mission, Jewish children in Germany, Austria, Czechoslovakia, and Poland were put on trains and sent, without their parents, to safety. Between 1938 and 1940, people in England, Wales, Northern Ireland, and Scotland took in nearly 10,000 children.

When German planes started to drop bombs over Britain, people there too wanted to keep their children safe. In England, it was decided that six cities, including London, were especially vulnerable to German bombs. Operation Pied Piper evacuated nearly 2 million children from these cities to villages and farms in safer locations. Wealthier parents made their own arrangements and sent their children off to live with relatives in the country, while others were sent across the ocean to the United States, Australia, and Canada.

ACKNOWLEDGMENTS

Dan Lafrance—for his patience.

Thanks always to editors Barbara Berson and Catherine Marjoribanks, to proofreader Judy Philips, and to Katie Hearn, Gayna Theophilus, Brigitte Waisberg, Monica Charny, Elaine Burns, and the rest of the crew at Annick Press.

Barbara Kissick, librarian and first friend on The Island. Kate Martin and Andrea Deveau, second and third friends, but who is counting?

All the Burkes—Kelly, Kirby, Taylor, Erica, and Cameron. Thomas and Margaret Whelan. All the Monthonys—Lolita, James, Eliana, Adrian. And to the McCauley Cheuys—Catherine, Dave, Brian, and Renee.

Linda Bellm, Ann Ball, Donna Patton, Shelley Grieve, Gail Advent Latouche. And then there is lunch: Julia Bell, Linda Holeman, Meg Masters.

Kathy Kacer, Marilyn Wise.

Readers in Holland: Eveline Vehaar, Marcella Hilde Rinske Verhaar-de Jong, Paula Verhaar-Jehee, and thanks to Ylva van Buuren.

Family, Dot and Gus, Sam, Joe, Kai, and David MacLeod, and beautiful Laurel too.

And Ada Wynston, Survivor, an inspiration for the present and future.